I0684813

Christmas Travelers

by

Wally White

Foreward by Della Reese

Edited by Mary Hicks

a Gray Faye Publishing

Gray Faye Publishing
grayfayepublishing@yahoo.com

ISBN-13: 978-0615549606 (Gray Faye Publishing)
ISBN-10: 0615549608

Cover Design by Sean Stearley and Jason Brown
Photography of Author by Barrett Gregory

Acknowledgements

To keep it short and simple, I should thank everyone I've ever known or crossed paths with – especially if I'm related to you; or I know you from Eden, Whipperwill Hills, Appalachian State, "Guiding Light," UP Church, UCSL, "Exit Speed," "Private Practice," or "The Mentalist."

However, I'll add a little more detail. I am in a constant state of gratitude for the family I was born into and the friends that surround me. My parents, Gray and Judy White, have always supported my decisions, even when I wanted to do things that were a little too "artsy" to make sense in the real world. They are responsible for my love of Christmas. They are responsible for my love of life.

There is a danger in listing names of people you wish to thank because it's a sure way of leaving off one or more names that should in all likelihood be mentioned first. That said, here it goes. I wish to thank – Della Reese for being my friend, spiritual mentor, and the inspiration of characters in many of my writing projects (including this one). Mary Hicks for your fantastic notes, and for being someone I've aspired to be like since I was a kid growing up hoping that one day I too could live in the big city and work in television. Brenda Nesbitt for putting Mary and I together on this project, and for being the other role model I hoped to grow up to be. Sean Stearley and Jason Brown giving me your time to develop a cover that elevated the whole project. Barrett Gregory for using me to test out your new camera. Sarah Cobb, Thad Rodgers, Jodi Smith, and Marc McTizic for offering guidance and assistance that made this book come to fruition as well as many other projects that came before this one. Shanelle Renet' for giving me the laptop that freed me from my desk and apartment so that writing, as well as Facebooking, could go on from behind the sets of a couple of said TV shows listed above … as well as my outside office, aka Starbucks. The Kennith White family (Ken, Amy, Hanson, and Larson), all of the Abe and Stella White lineage, and all of the Walsey and Myrtle Whitaker lineage for being the basis of my first connotations of Christmas. Anna Muirhead Motley "Mo" Burton for sharing with me a great love of Christmas and the many great stories that can be told about it. Kelly Jo Eldredge for the many calls and emails filled with advice. Brendalyn Richard and Sarah Pryzibilla for keeping me employed so that I could concentrate on writing this book instead of worrying about silly things like eating and sleeping under a roof. Melissa Hayden for not laughing too loudly at me for listening to Christmas music on hot summer days to stay in the holiday spirit. Patricia Cassell for our 23 Christmas Eve breakfasts and many other wonderful memories. Lynn Smith for leaving a mark on my heart that will forever be a part of all my celebrations. And to a sweet, white, fluffy little girl named Ginger whose purr puts me to sleep most nights.

AND if you bought a copy of this, my very first book, I thank you most of all. Please put your name at the top of the list. Well … right after my parents.

Foreward

Christmas Travelers is a marvelous experience. It's full of the real things about Christmas. It's not just about wrapped gifts and Christmas trees and bows and ribbons. It is about people, who never knew each other before they boarded this coach flight, trying to get home to what they think they know as Christmas.

What they discover is the real meaning of Christmas. As they travel, they create a magnificent family with each other. There is a wonderful child, with a real shining star that gives the light to lead the way. With lovers, with friends, with joy, with a certain peace, they get a whole new understanding of what Christmas is really about.

I so enjoyed being a part of this story. I'm sure you'll love it too, because the elements that it brings together are what Christmas is really meant to be.

Della Reese

Chapter 1

Night in the desert gives a feeling of cool stillness by sight alone. That is especially true on this winter night. The soft, white light of the moon illumines dunes of sand. Polka-dotted with stars upon stars, the sky is clear. It is a landscape befitting of the nativity story.

The gentle breeze goes without notice. It is seemingly on an endless journey marked from one solitary cactus to another through a place unscathed by modern society. The stream of air is only strong enough to gather particles of sand. The serenity is both peaceful and yet lonely. In the distance, the view softly shifts. Much in the same way that the dark ocean becomes one with the light blue sky on a summer day, here the black sky blends together with a light gray hue coming up from the ground.

As the breeze and the sand particles move over one last dune, there are sparkling lights in a valley. It is a city alone in the desert.

Phoenix, Arizona – December 23

A neighborhood is alive with people stirring about. The yards have equal portions of perfectly groomed sod separated by driveways. Houses are adorned with a variety of Christmas themed garage doors. Some are painted with famous cartoon characters wearing Santa hats, while others are host to museum worthy abstract art. A live nativity scene, including a new mother with her baby wrapped in a fleece blanket to mock the swaddling clothes, draws large crowds of children wanting to pet the donkeys and sheep. People are dressed in a myriad of styles ranging from full-on winter coats to shorts and T-shirts.

Christmas trees and electric candles beam through windows. Roofs are outlined with gleaming plastic icicles. Small motors hum as they power fans that inflate fabric statues of polar bears, Christmas presents, and a team of Santas on motorcycles that are lit from within. Even strong, sturdy cactuses stand tall … with blinking multi-colored lights wrapped from bottom to top.

Then there is the Carpenter home. Sitting in the middle of the block, it stands out from all the other houses. Among all the themes, lights, and electric currents being used, this is the house that gets the strangest looks, furrowed brows, and frowns. Its Christmas theme is – nothing. No lights. No sparkle. No moving reindeer. Nothing.

Inside, Charley Carpenter arrives home carrying an armful of groceries. He is 24-years-old, five foot eight inches tall, and bone straight skinny. His low-grade suit, shirt, and tie are ill fitted, but well serve the purpose of looking professional for his repossession job at the bank. The living room is dark except for flickering lights coming from the TV. He calls out, "Hey Sweetie. How was your day?"

Holly Carpenter lies on the sofa with her messy hair pulled into a ponytail. She too is 24-years-old, but avoids further description because of her oversized sweatshirt and sweatpants that are pulled in multiple directions. She doesn't answer him, but instead raises the remote control to continue flipping channels on the TV.

"You haven't turned on the Christmas lights," he says as he unloads the bags from his arms onto the floor and hits a light switch. The Christmas tree comes to life as well as two electric candles that glow through a closed curtain behind the tree, and a set of white tree lights tacked around the room's ceiling. He opens the curtains.

"We want to let our new neighbors know we've done something to participate in their festival. We should go walk around and look at everybody's stuff in a bit. They've done some real pretty decorating out there."

She continues her channel surfing without responding to him.

He takes the bags from the floor and puts them on the coffee table in front of her. Sitting down next to her, he says, "I have something that's going to make you happy." She remains locked on the TV.

"Got a little piece of home for ya," he adds.

Her face brightens up. "Did Momma send me something?"

"What's your favorite treat?" he asks.

"Oh my God. Momma sent me some white chocolate peanut butter crackers?" she exclaims.

His face twitches. "Well, no. But ..."

"She sent white chocolate pretzels, then?" she substitutes.

"She didn't actually send anything, but I got you some white chocolate pretzels. Well, kind of." Charley pulls one of the grocery bags onto the sofa between them. "I thought we'd make them together." He adds a wink to seal the deal.

Holly's face loses signs of excitement. "No mail from Momma?"

"You know she thinks she can't do nothing outside of her little piece of Arkansas. But let's bring her to us with this here food. What do you say?" he asks with his best effort to pick her up out of a funk.

Charley coaxes Holly off the sofa. When she stands, we see her very large pregnant belly as it pushes her sweatshirt away from the pants. He guides her into the kitchen, which is only separated from the living room by a breakfast bar. She squints when he hits the light switch. The room is absent of any personal touches that make a house a home.

While a slightly more energized Holly gets out the double boiler from a cabinet, Charley sorts out the groceries on the bar. "I'll start breaking up these chocolate bricks," he says.

"You can if you want to, but you should have the wax ready to go too," she instructs.

"Wax?" he asks.

"Yeah," she adds as though he just asked the most ridiculous question.

"You mean like wax paper to lay the pretzels on?"

"No. The paraffin wax to make the chocolate stick to the pretzel," she explains.

He pauses. "It'll stick without that, won't it?" he asks while trying to cover his desperation that she says yes.

"You forgot the wax?" she asks feeling the dismay rolling back in.

"No. I didn't forget it. I didn't even know about it. I mean, who knew wax was edible?" he adds with a hint of "duh" in his undertone.

Holly's smile drops. No fading to a frown. It drops immediately into a look of outright misery. "Nothing's going to make this Christmas right. My family's not here. We're like 1,500 miles away from anybody we know. We can't do nothing we'd normally do. And it's hot. It's hot at Christmas. I hate this place."

She hurries out of the kitchen, down the hallway, into the bathroom, and slams the door behind her.

* * * * * * *

A phone hangs on the wall of an empty kitchen lit by one bulb above the stove. It begins to ring. The room is painted a traditional kitchen yellow. A pristine folded dishtowel lies next to the sink on an immaculate countertop.

The phone keeps ringing, and ringing … and ringing. It seems impossible that the call hasn't gone to voicemail yet.

Nellie Goldman, a heavyset black woman in her late 70's, slowly rounds the corner. The continuing rings don't seem to give her any added motivation to move faster at all. She finally makes it to the phone. Still with no sense of hurry whatsoever, she slowly picks up the handset and brings it to her ear.

"Hello," she answers.

On the other end of the phone is Opal, Nellie's slightly younger sister who is beyond annoyed by this point.

"I kept thinking your answering machine was going to pick up," she spouts off.

"What answering machine?" Nellie asks.

"I was standing in the post office the day Phillip sent it to you," Opal shoots back.

"I don't know nothing 'bout no answering machine. When I'm here, I'll talk to you. When I'm not, I won't. Is that what you were calling about? To check up on an answering machine?" Nellie asks defiantly.

Opal settles back in her chair. She shifts to a more relaxed position. "No. I was calling to see if you're packed and ready to go."

Nellie rolls her eyes. "For what?"

Opal straightens back up again as her brow tightens. "You know you're coming to Detroit tomorrow to celebrate

Christmas with us." She shakes her head. "I knew you were going to do this. Look, I know you got the plane ticket. I saw your signature on the shipper's website," she says with great confidence.

"Am I supposed to believe you even know how to go onto a website?" Nellie asks, knowing her sister knows every bit as much about the laws of physics as she does about turning on a computer.

"The point is that I know you got that ticket. Now, are you …?"

"Aunt Nellie," a gentle male voice interrupts Opal.

Nellie's demeanor changes. Her face softens. She settles into a nearby kitchen chair. Sweetly she says, "Hey baby. You ready for Christmas?"

"I don't know. Are you coming?" he asks. Her great nephew, Opal's grandson, Phillip, has commandeered the phone away from his grandmother. He is a handsome, 37-year-old, light skinned black man who obviously spends a fair amount of time at his local gym. He is the apple of his Aunt Nellie's eye, and he knows it.

Nellie quickly reworks her approach as to why she has no plans of coming to Detroit. "You know ever since your Uncle Albert passed, it's hard for me to do a lot of traveling."

"Aunt Nellie, please come. You still haven't met my son. He's three now. It's the first Christmas that he's excited about Santa and all the gifts. I want you to be here to share in that," he pleads.

"Well …" Nellie struggles to get past her favorite nephew's request. Then she's inspired by a new excuse. "Did you see the plane ticket your grandmother sent? I'd have to fly from Arizona to New Jersey, and then back to Michigan. It just doesn't even make sense," she jabs at her sister.

"I know. I didn't have a choice," he says.

"You?" Nellie asks.

"The direct flights only had first class seats left. And I know you're probably used to flying first class, but I couldn't afford it," he explains.

"You bought the ticket? You didn't have to do that. I could've paid for my own ticket," she says.

Phillip smiles. He knows he just hooked her into making the trip. "I wanted to do it. That's how important it is to me. So, are you coming?" he asks already knowing the answer.

"I'll see you tomorrow," she concedes.

"I have a car service picking you up at 4:30am," he adds.

"Now that's too much. I can get myself to the airport."

"The reservation is non-refundable," he says. "See you tomorrow." Before she can respond, Phillip hangs up.

Nellie looks at the phone, shakes her head, and hangs up as well.

* * * * * * *

On a little girl's bed is a pink princess suitcase packed full of stuffed animals. A giant blue bear seemingly floats toward the bed. As he arrives, he rises above the suitcase. His power of flight is revealed. Alonya Walker, a 7-year-old Hispanic girl, is busy packing all the essentials for her upcoming trip.

Her father, Frank Walker, enters the room. He is a forty-year-old balding white guy that stands five foot eleven inches tall with green eyes. In fact, the only thing he can point to, as proof that he is Alonya's father, is her green eyes.

"We've got to get up early in the morning. It's time for bed," he says.

"I just have to pack a few more things," Alonya insists.

Frank looks at the suitcase packed so full with stuffed animals that there is no chance of closing the case. "Honey, you can't take all those."

She looks at him as though he's just said the most ridiculous thing ever stated in the history of the English language. "But I won't have anything to play with at Nana and Papa's."

"Your grandparents have plenty for you to do. Before I became this handsome adult you see before you, I too was once a kid, you know. And when I was a kid, I lived in that house. I played with toys all the time, and I'm sure some of them are still there," he adds.

"I can't play with boy toys Daddy. I mean Army men can't have tea," she concludes.

He smiles imagining the suggestion. "I'm sure your Nana will see to it that all the proper tea participants will be there for you. Besides you'll get lots of new toys for Christmas."

"What if Santa comes here? He may not know how to find Nana and Papa's house since no kids live there," she says revealing what has been worrying her all along.

"Santa knows how to find you. I promise. Now where is your real suitcase? The one that I packed?"

She points to a fully packed suitcase behind the door. Frank attempts unsuccessfully to close the animal case.

"Have you brushed your teeth yet?" he asks. She nods her head.

He takes the still opened case off the bed and places it on the floor. Then he picks up Alonya and puts her in bed. He gently pulls the covers up and kisses her on the cheek.

"Get some sleep. We'll be getting up in just a few hours to go to the airport," he says. He picks up the animal case. "I'll get this carry-on bag closed. Some of your tea guests will have to come out, but I'll make sure your favorites are there."

"Make sure that ..." she starts to instruct.

"I'll take care of it. Go to sleep," he says. Frank turns off the lights with his arm as he exits the room balancing the overflowing case of stuffed tea party guests with both of his hands.

In the hallway, Frank stops in front of a framed picture hanging on the wall. It is Alonya, a beautiful Hispanic woman, who is clearly Alonya's mom, and himself. They are in a park. Alonya is in her mom's lap, and her mom is sitting in Frank's lap. The picture is electrified by what must have been a loud, boisterous laugh coming from all three of them. With his arms still full carrying the animal suitcase, Frank leans in and touches his forehead to the frame. He stays there for a lingering moment. Then he straightens up, and walks away.

* * * * * * *

The grounds of the Phoenix Wellness Spa are serene. A slight breeze blows through the palms. Water trickles through a man-made creek with mini-waterfalls that leads to one giant fall into the spa's swimming pool.

Inside, the office of Jacq Murphy is mostly quiet except for the rapid clicks coming from her computer keyboard. The room is only lit by her desk light, which illuminates papers strewn about in a way that would make it nearly impossible for anyone except her to find any needed information. The clicks go silent. With her brown, shoulder length hair almost touching the desk, Jacq is face deep in a notebook. While her blue eyes remain locked on her reading material, her fair skinned hand reaches for a pen.

An older, slightly overweight man stops at her office door. "I thought I was the only sucker left in the sales department tonight," he says.

She barely looks up as she responds, "I'll be here for a while getting all this ready."

"Tomorrow's Christmas Eve. All the work will be here when we get back on the 27th. Give yourself a break," he suggests.

"Can't. I've got to get this presentation ready for the last minute pitch in New York tomorrow," she says.

"You're the one who took that meeting? I thought the boss was taking it himself, so he could go see the Rockettes. All he was talking about this afternoon was those eighteen perfect legs kicking into the air at the same time," he says with a laugh. Jacq finally stops reading. She looks up at her co-worker clearly annoyed.

"My wife would've killed me for taking the assignment," he stammers.

"His wife must've talked to yours then," she says. "Lucky for all you hard working guys, this girl isn't tied down with a family."

"Well, at least you'll get a couple of days in New York on the boss' dime. Have fun in the city that never sleeps. I hear there's no place better to be this time of year," he adds.

"Top sales aren't made by turning business trips into vacations. I'll fly back tomorrow night as soon as I get a signature on the contract. The faster it gets filed, the faster I get my commission and move on to the next client," she proclaims.

"You're a machine. Merry Christmas then," he says as he walks away. Jacq suddenly finds the information she's been searching for in the paperwork. She starts typing again.

Chapter 2

December 24

Holly has her face buried deep into her pillow. She is sleeping as sound as a woman can in the final days of pregnancy. The room is completely dark except for the blue glow coming from the bedside clock. It reads 4:00am.

A light comes on suddenly in the hallway. Charley enters the bedroom still wearing the shirt and pants that he arrived home from work in. He turns on the lamp next to Holly. She reacts with a grunt and a few flinches, but doesn't readily come completely out of her sleep. He gently shakes her.

"Sweetie, wake up," he says.

She slowly opens her eyes with a few more grunts throughout the process. As she rolls onto her back, "What?" she complains.

"Get up and pack a bag," he says while taking a suitcase out of the closet.

Holly sits up now fully awake. "Pack? For what?" she asks while rubbing the sleepy out of her eyes.

Charley plops the empty suitcase onto the foot of the bed. He grabs a couple pairs of pants, some T-shirts, and a sweater from the closet. "I booked us a flight home. We need to be at the airport by five," he says while continuing to pull a few pairs of underwear and socks from a drawer. With his hands full, he drops it all into the suitcase.

"Really? How did you get off work?" she asks with a mixture of giddiness and shock.

"I just told them I have to go home. Now, get up. We need to leave here as soon as possible if we're going to be on time," he says while starting to pull together sets of underwear for Holly. "Is this okay?" he holds up a fancy red lace bra.

Holly looks down at her oversized, clean but stained nightshirt. "Um no, I don't think that one fits right now." She gives herself one good shove up off the bed. "I'll get what I need," she says as she takes the bra from him. "How much were the last minute tickets?"

"Don't worry about it. Hurry up and pack," he says as he walks out of the room.

Holly puts the red bra back in the drawer, and instead takes out larger, much less fancy underwear. Charley comes back into the room carrying an overcoat. "Is this okay for you?"

She looks at the full length black down coat. "Where'd you get that? I thought I left that at Momma's since I'd never need it here," she asks.

Charley looks at the coat, then at his wife. "I don't know. It was in the closet. Is it okay? We need to get you packed so we can go," he urges.

"Yes, it's fine. I just didn't know it was here. I'll be ready in a few minutes, but you're going to have to give me a minute to go to the bathroom," she says. She stops to inspect what he's wearing. "Isn't that what you wore yesterday?" she asks.

"Yeah, I guess I never got around to changing," he says. He pulls his half-buttoned shirt over his shoulders and tosses it on top of a pile of other clothes on the closet floor. He pulls out an old sweatshirt that he would normally wear to lie around watching the weekend games on TV.

"Honey, put on something nicer than that. It is Christmas Eve," Holly requests.

As Holly moves past him, Charley throws the sweatshirt on top of the ever-growing closet pile. He takes out a red sweater from the back corner of his closet shelf. "Do you need me to pack anything else for you? We need to go as soon as you get out of the bathroom," he says with a bit of urgency in his tone.

"I can't hear you if you're talking to me," she calls out from behind the closed door.

* * * * * * *

15

In the Walker's house, Alonya sits at the kitchen table in front of a bowl of cereal. She is more interested in watching the local news than in eating. Frank enters rolling their suitcases behind him, which he has linked together so that he need only pull one. Of course he also has Alonya's pink princess carry-on roller bag that is sure to test the bag size leniency of the airport security guards.

"There's no time for television this morning. We've got to get to the airport," he says.

Alonya stops mid-spoon entry. "I wish my birthday was tomorrow like Jesus," she says.

He stops. With a slight chuckle he asks, "What?"

"Tomorrow is Jesus' birthday. That means he got birthday and Christmas gifts on the same day," she concludes.

He reaches over and turns off the television. "Not exactly, but I get where you're going with that. You get just as many gifts. Yours just comes twice a year instead of all on one day. Now, finish eating. We need to go," he says while heading out the door with the suitcases.

She shovels in a spoonful of cereal into her mouth. "I was watching the news for the weather report like Mom used to do," she says.

"We live in Arizona. It's going to be sunny and warm. Finish your cereal and go brush your teeth. We need to be in the car driving toward the airport in five minutes," he instructs from outside.

* * * * * * *

16

Outside of Nellie's front door, a man in a driver's uniform rings the doorbell. There is no response. He tries to look in through a nearby window, but all the lights are off. There are no signs of anyone that is awake and ready to be taken anywhere. The man takes his cell phone out of his pocket. He selects "Work" from his speed dial list. After only one ring, someone answers on the other end.

"Yeah, it's Ed again. What do you want me to do? I rang the doorbell for the last ten minutes. If the lady's in there, she's either deaf or dead. Plus, there's not even any lights on. Are you sure this is the right address?" he asks for the third time this morning. "Okay, one more time. Then, I'm out of here."

He hangs up the phone clearly annoyed that he's been asked to make another futile attempt at getting someone to come to the door. "Got up for nothing. Could be sleeping right now," he mutters to himself as he rings the doorbell. "One, two, three, four, five, six, seven, eight, nine, ten. I'm out of here," he turns to leave. He gets about halfway back to his car on the sidewalk leading away from the front door when a light comes on from the driveway side of the house. He stops when he hears the lock turn and then the door open.

"Good morning," Nellie calls out. "Come around to the side door." The driver shakes his head, exhales, and then turns around.

He enters into the kitchen. "Ms. Goldman?"

"It's Mrs.," she calls out from the other room. "My suitcase is there by the door if you want to take it out." He sees her black roller suitcase with a lavender ribbon tied around the handle sitting next to the door. Still a little disappointed that he didn't get away, he takes her bag outside.

Nellie enters the kitchen dressed as though she's headed to a sophisticated holiday party. Her hair is perfectly styled with the mix of black and gray soft curls landing just above her shoulder. Her dark green pants and matching green satin blouse are highlighted by the sparkling red and green poinsettia pendent that is hanging on a long 14-karat gold necklace, a matching poinsettia ring, and a wrist full of diamond, emerald, and ruby bracelets. She's added the surprise of a subtle pair of red and green wrestler styled sneakers nestled under the pant hem. And to cap it off, she's ready for Detroit's cold weather in her white, black, and gray full-length chinchilla fur coat.

She places a Christmas card on the counter. After getting a pen out of a nearby drawer, Nellie begins to write a note. The driver comes back into the kitchen. "Sorry. I should've asked if there was anything else," he says. With a slight grunt letting him know he interrupted a thought, she keeps writing. He stands at attention with his hands crossed in front of him waiting not so patiently for her to finish her note. When she finishes writing, she places the card in its envelope, and then the envelope on top of a cake wrapped in green cellophane.

Nellie hands the cake with card on top to the driver. "Run this across the street for me," she asks without a question mark.

His head does a momentary shake with genuine confusion. He looks at the cake, and then back to her. "Excuse me?"

18

"Take the cake to my neighbor across the street," she says while putting the pen back in the drawer.

"It's a quarter to five in the morning," he suggests with a bit of baffled shock.

"I know what time it is," she says.

"Ms .... Mrs. Goldman, we're running late to the airport," he says while trying to hand the cake back to her.

She looks at the cake, and then turns to the sink where she puts lotion on her hands from a bottle sitting perfectly aligned with the hand soap. "Then stop wasting time and hurry the cake across the street," she says without looking up. "I'll be behind you."

Outside, Nellie locks the door as the driver makes his way back to the car from the neighbor's house. A sweet gray-haired lady, fully dressed, waves. "Thanks for the cake, Nellie. Have a good trip," she says.

"I will," Nellie says as she waves back. She looks to the driver. "I told you she'd be up."

Finally, she is almost to the car. The driver opens the back door. Nellie veers away from the car toward a newspaper lying on the driveway. She picks it up. "I called last night and told them to hold the paper through the holidays. You want this one," she offers it to the driver.

He reluctantly takes the paper and throws it in the front passenger seat. The headline reads, "White Christmas headed to the Northeast." "Sure, thanks. Mrs. Goldman, we really have to get going," he urges her.

"Okay, okay. I'll get in the car if you'll get out of the way," she barks back. He steps further away from the door. She gets in. "My bag is in the trunk, isn't it?" she asks.

"Yes. Your bag is in the trunk," he says while closing the door. With it firmly closed he mumbles, "Shoulda put you in there too."

* * * * * * *

As Jacq closes her laptop and places it in her briefcase, a woman wearing blue scrubs stops in her doorway. "What are you doing here so early?" she asks.

Jacq looks up to see Erin standing there. Erin is a massage therapist at the spa. She and Jacq have known each other since high school. A closer look at Jacq's desk reveals a picture of five girls – Jacq and Erin being two of them.

"Try *so late*," Jacq answers. "Haven't been home since yesterday morning."

"When are you going to find a husband that you have to get home to?" Erin asks with a special grin. "Neither one of us party the way we did back in the day. I can't imagine life anymore that doesn't include me rushing home to a meal laid out on the table prepared by my man."

Jacq gathers her things to leave. "I've told you many times, you nabbed a special one. They don't all cook. But either way, maybe I'll find one in New York."

"New York? When are you going there?" Erin asks.

"No time like the present," she answers holding up her things indicating her departure. "Boss got a call yesterday from an old client. They're looking for ways to keep the employees happy while still holding out on raises and stock options. Enter the Phoenix Wellness Spa retreat."

"Great. We'll relax them and send them back home to the hustle and bustle of the Big Apple telling all their friends and family how great we are. But it's Christmas Eve. I know we are servicing clients that are here for their holiday vacations, but can't a business pitch wait until the first of the year?"

"Nope. He's got money that he needs to spend before the end of the year, and he said today was his only day to meet. So since his call yesterday afternoon, I've been pulling together the pitch that normally takes several days. Gotta give the client what he wants if I'm going to get him to give me what I want. And who knows, maybe I'll meet that man you keep talking about while I'm at it," she says as she leaves her office.

"Two thousand miles away and unavailable for day to day contact?" Erin calls out.

"Unavailable men are my specialty," Jacq retorts.

* * * * * * *

The early morning sky appears more night than day as Charley and Holly approach the airport. The peaceful, calm air gives signs of a city that is still sleeping. But with one last turn, the airport traffic is a drastic shift. Flashing turn signals blink both right and left as some cars attempt to pull away from the same drop off zones that others are pushing their way into.

Charley finds his airline terminal and pulls the car to the curb. He gets out of the car, takes the suitcase out of the trunk, and then comes around to open the door for Holly. She looks at him with pure confusion. "What are you doing? You can't just park the car here," she says.

"I'm going to go park, but I didn't want you to have to walk so far," he explains. "Get on out before security comes to make me move."

It takes her a moment to get positioned just right for the exit. Once there she looks up at Charley, who is still standing by the opened door. He reaches in. Holly grabs his elbow with both of her hands, and he pulls her up and out.

With a bit of a whimper she says, "I'm sorry you're suddenly married to a circus elephant. I'm not that cute high school cheerleader you fell in love with anymore."

"You are exactly who I fell in love with. Soon that baby's going to be ready to come out, and when he or she does, I don't care if you lose a pound or gain 100 more. I love you," he reassures her.

He takes her in his arms and gives her a gentle hug that has all the bells and whistles of the very best security blanket. She touches his cheek and stretches over her pregnant belly that separates them to kiss him. As their lips meet … a police siren quips, followed by an officer calling out on his loud speaker that the car needs to be moved. Charley snaps into gear. "Right," he says. "Go wait inside that door. I'll be back as quick as possible," he instructs her. He rushes around the car to the driver's side, but before getting in, he throws his hand in the air to the officer. "Merry Christmas," he offers. "This is going to be the best Christmas ever."

Holly is filled with joy as she watches him drive away. She collects the roll away luggage and makes her way inside.

Before Holly gets fully in the building, a parking shuttle pulls up to the curb. Frank helps Alonya off before he carries their luggage off. There are the two suitcases packed with clothes that had to be unlinked for bus storage, his over the shoulder carry-on bag with reading material for the trip, and then of course Alonya's special princess bag.

"Daddy, can I pull my bag?" she asks.

"Yes, that would be a big help," he replies. She takes the handle of the princess bag and begins to walk toward the entrance, but Frank calls out for her to wait as he is still working on getting all wheels pointed in the same direction to pull the two remaining bags, plus balance his other bag on his shoulder just right. Finally situated, Frank and Alonya make their way into the building.

Inside, Frank has punched all the necessary buttons at the self check-in kiosk, paid to check the two bags, shown his I.D. to the airline attendant, and is now in line to hand the bags over to be scanned before they are sent to the plane. The security officer asks all the normal questions. Frank confirms that the bags have been in his possession the whole time since being packed, there are no locks on the bags, and the contents do not include any weapons or flammable liquids – though that question did spark a concern. If someone were indeed knowingly passing off luggage with weapons and/or flammable liquids, would this simple question be the way to slip them up and get a confession?

Not being a security expert, he wondered if this tactic had ever worked because years ago when walking back into San Diego after spending the afternoon in Tijuana, the same security method was being used. One by one, American citizens would show their driver's license, and were then each asked, "Are you a citizen of the United States?" Frank had thought then, if someone has taken the time to travel from wherever they may have started, had a fake driver's license made, stood in line behind countless people being asked the same question – with EVERYONE giving the same affirmative answer – would this be the trick question that foiled their plan to sneak across the boarder? It seems like criminals with mal-intent would've started by mastering the fib, but here years later airports across the nation are using the same basic questioning technique in the name of security.

Happily in this case, Frank is not said criminal telling a fib, but in fact the most dangerous thing packed in these cases is perhaps a bad combination of planned outfits. Luckily he has a loving mother waiting in D.C. more than ready to prove her good credit score as soon as she can get her granddaughter to a mall.

As Frank and Alonya start to walk away, the security officer sees that Alonya is pulling her princess bag. "You don't trust me with the pretty bag?" he jokes.

Alonya answers, "My friends are in here. They can't ride under the plane."

The security officer perks up, suddenly concerned by her answer. Frank puts his hand up. "Stuffed animals," he says. The officer huffs back down, and turns to take the next waiting passenger's bag.

In the security line, Nellie has made her way to the front. She places her purse in one of the bins, puts it on the conveyor belt and starts to walk through the metal detector, but is stopped by a guard. "Ma'am, you have to take off your shoes," the woman barks. The guard then catches a glimpse of Nellie's sparkling wrist full of bracelets. "Your jewelry will have to come off too."

"For what?" Nellie asks.

"For your security," the guard answers.

"Can you not tell the difference between diamonds and weapons?" Nellie retorts.

The guard points to the stack of bins, and then walks away to another line of people. Nellie is none too happy about this task. Nor are the people behind her, who have to wait while she takes off her many possible security risks in need of being x-rayed. She puts her necklace, earrings, bracelets, and shoes in a bin. As that bin starts down the conveyor belt, Nellie turns to walk through the metal detector again. "Ma'am, your coat will have to go on the conveyor belt," a different guard barks out.

"I beg your pardon?" Nellie responds.

"Put your coat on the conveyor belt," the guard orders.

"Surely, you don't think this chinchilla is going on that. You'll have to find another way," she says with her own spark of attitude.

Moments later, Nellie is standing sans chinchilla on the other side of the metal detector with her arms and legs spread out as the guard runs the hand held metal detector up and down her entire body.

Over at the gate, Charley finds two seats together in the waiting area. He sets their carry-on bag in one seat, and helps Holly into the other one. "Sit here with the stuff, and I'll go get us something to eat," he says.

"Okay. Just remember I'm not supposed to have any caffeine. So I'll take a Sprite instead of Coke, and then whatever kind of breakfast sandwich you can find with sausage in it," she answers.

Holly stretches her legs out and lays her head back attempting to lie down in a sitting position. Jacq, carrying only her briefcase with her laptop, sits in the seat next to the bag Charley left behind. She closes her eyes and takes a deep breath. This is perhaps the first moment she's taken to breathe since getting word about the New York pitch yesterday afternoon. The ring of a cell phone interrupts her short respite. She reaches in both of her pockets, and then digs through her briefcase to find her phone. It wasn't the one ringing, however. It seems Charley has the same ring.

Jacq leans over to a resting Holly. "Excuse me. I think your cell phone is ringing."

A confused Holly raises her head and looks at Jacq. "What cell phone?" Holly asks.

"It sounds like it's coming from that bag," Jacq says while pointing at Charley's bag.

Realizing that Jacq isn't a crazy lady talking nonsense, Holly finally snaps to it. She reaches with a little extra effort to get to the phone. Just as she pulls it out of the bag, it stops ringing. She starts to open the flip phone, but is interrupted by Charley running back over.

"Who are you calling?" he asks.

"Nobody. Somebody just called, but I didn't get to it in time. I was just checking to see who it was," she says.

He exchanges the phone for the bag of food he has returned with. "It was probably the airline confirming our last minute purchase or something. I'll take care of it while you eat," he says.

He turns to walk away. "Where are you going?" Holly asks.

"To take care of the phone call like I just said," he answers.

"Just do it here, and watch the bag and the food. I need to go to the bathroom," she says as she struggles up and out of the chair.

Jacq watches the couple's exchange from the corner of her eye, and then starts reading a vacation magazine. Holly waddles off towards the restroom. Charley puts the phone in his pocket, sits, and takes one of the sandwiches out of the bag. Having just heard him tell his wife that he was calling the airline, Jacq finds it odd that the phone was so quickly put away.

"If you need to make a private call, but have to stay here with your things, I can move," she offers.

"Oh, that's okay. It was nothing," he says. "Thank you though. That's real nice. People outside of the south usually aren't that kind."

Jacq smiles and goes back to reading her magazine. Nellie walks up at this same time looking for a seat. She's about to sit down when the announcement comes over the loud speaker that boarding is beginning for priority customers and people who need extra time. Without a beat, Nellie turns from the empty seat and heads over to the gate.

A short time later, Charley is pacing when Holly finally makes it back. "They started boarding. Hurry up. We've got to get on the plane," he says nervously.

"Sorry. I didn't realize it was time. I can only move so fast you know," she explains.

They arrive at the gate. Charley gives the attendant both of their boarding passes. She runs them through the scanner and hands them back to Charley. They make their way down the ramp. But as they enter the plane, the greeting flight attendant stops them.

"Wait. I'm sorry. Did anyone ask you when you are due?" he asks.

"Why does that matter?" Holly asks.

"It's just that you look like you're pretty far along. We have to make sure that you are cleared for travel, and that you're not in danger of going into labor mid-flight," he answers.

"She's seven months," Charley darts in with an answer. "And she's a little sensitive about her size," he adds with a whisper. The attendant nods and steps out of their way.

"Why did you just lie to that man?" Holly asks.

He puts his arm around Holly and encourages her to start walking. "He wasn't going to let you on the plane," he answers. "We need to stick to that story until we get home today. Remember, seven months, and you're sensitive about your size."

"You just said you didn't care if I gained another 100 pounds," she says.

"Babe, I don't, but apparently they do. Let's just get home," he suggests.

The plane seating has three seats on each side. Charley and Holly arrive at row 18. Nellie is sitting in the aisle seat. Holly looks at the posted seating chart, and back at the boarding passes. She looks at Charley. "You didn't get me the aisle seat? I'm going to spend the whole flight climbing over this lady to go to the bathroom," she says with great dismay.

"I didn't really have a choice, sweetie. We're lucky to even get to sit together at all," he says.

"It really isn't a problem," Nellie says without invitation. "I'll just slide over to the window seat."

"You'd do that?" Charley asks.

Nellie smiles and slides over the two seats. Charley sits in the middle seat, while Holly settles into her requested spot. Nellie looks out the window, but then back at Charley. "I'm pretty sure you'll have to get up for me once or twice for my own trip to the ladies room," she adds.

"Not a problem. I can't thank you enough for sliding over," he says.

Holly leans over him. "Thanks. I'm feeling kind of stressed. This was a last minute trip. I didn't even know about it 'til like three hours ago," she says.

"Well, the pilot is going to fly the plane. So all you have to do now is sit back and relax," Nellie reassures Holly.

Frank and Alonya run onto the plane getting there just before the attendants close the door. They make their way back to row 17 and take the aisle and middle seats. Alonya sits next to Jacq, who is already buckled in and reading notes for the pitch. She has her overhead light on, and the shade pulled down.

The plane backs up from the gate as the attendants take their last pass making sure everything is closed up and that the passengers are complying with regulations of having everything tucked away. After making their way to the runway, the pilot calls for the attendants to take their seats. The plane speeds up. Jacq continues reading her notes undaunted. Frank puts his arm around Alonya, who hugs in as close as she can get with the armrest pulled down. Behind them, Holly clasps her hands together and begins whispering the Lord's Prayer while Charley rubs her back. Nellie chuckles, looks out the window and says, "Thanks God for another safe flight."

Holly, having not heard Nellie, concludes with, "Dear God. Please don't crash this plane." Charley gently takes her hand into his. The plane lifts from the ground.

Chapter 3

After making it to the desired altitude, the pilot turns off the seat belt sign but announces that everyone should continue wearing it when seated. Holly gets up immediately and heads back to the lavatory. Frank lowers the tray in front of Alonya and takes some food out of his bag.

Alonya is too pre-occupied staring at Jacq to notice the food. As if she was holding her breath, she finally spits out, "Excuse me." Jacq is engrossed in the work she's doing on her laptop and doesn't hear her. So Alonya says again louder, "Excuse me."

"Alonya," Frank scolds his daughter. "Eat your snack."

"I just want her to raise the shade so I can see the clouds," Alonya explains.

Jacq looks up. "Sorry. The light from the window creates too much of a glare on my computer screen," she says before going back to work.

Alonya continues to stare at Jacq. Frank can see that wheels are turning in his determined little girl's brain. He attempts to distract her. "Honey, why don't we read one of your books," he offers.

"No thanks," she says not looking away from Jacq.

"You want me to get a couple of your stuffed animals out?" he asks.

"Nah. They would just want to look out the window too," she says. Jacq smiles, but keeps working. Alonya leans in toward her, "Have you ever flown before? The clouds are always so beautiful this high up," she suggests.

Frank snaps at his precocious daughter, "Alonya. Leave her alone."

Jacq's smile grows, but she remains focused on her work. Alonya takes another shot at correcting this window situation. "You know, I could switch seats with you if you want. That way the sun wouldn't get on your computer."

Breaking away from her work, Jacq explains, "That's a sweet offer, but adults generally avoid the middle seat if they can help it." She refocuses on her work thinking it is resolved.

"That's easy," Alonya retorts. "If you switch with me, my Dad can switch with you. Then you'll have the aisle seat. I see lots of adults in those seats."

"Alonya," Frank calls out. "You are seriously going to get grounded on Christmas Eve if you don't leave her alone."

"Actually," Jacq speaks up, "if you are willing to give me your seat, I'm fine with Alonya's proposal."

"What's a proposal?" Alonya asks.

Ignoring her, Frank asks Jacq, "Are you sure?"

Jacq nods. The deal has been successfully negotiated. Frank moves his bag under the seat in front of Alonya. He and Alonya then slide out into the aisle. Jacq moves her bag under the seat in front of her new spot, and then slides out into the aisle as well. Alonya happily pounces across the empty row into her newly acquired window seat, where the shade is promptly raised. Frank thanks Jacq with an awkward smile and then slides into his new middle seat home. Before Jacq settles in to her new spot, Holly comes up behind her.

"Hey, you're the nice lady that tried to help me get that call before," she says.

Jacq turns to see her. "Yes I am. Hello again."

"Idn't that funny that we were sitting together out there, and here we are one row apart on the plane?" Holly says.

Not as bemused by it, "Yes, it is quite a coincidence," Jacq admits before sitting.

The plane hits a little turbulence. Holly squeals, and falls into her seat. "It's okay," Charley offers some comfort. "Just get settled and put your seatbelt back on."

She extends the seatbelt to open it up as much as possible. "This thing is not comfortable around the two of us in this seat," she says. She has it extended as far as it will go, but only gets it to buckle by lowering the seatbelt under her pregnant belly.

"Are you sure that's okay for the baby?" Charley asked.

Now even more distress, "I think so. I don't know. It's not like I can ask him or her. I mean nothing's hurting from inside. It's just uncomfortable," Holly explains.

Without saying a word, Nellie reaches up and presses the service button. Neither Charley nor Holly notices because they are focused on finding a good position for her to sit safely, but with some bit of comfort. The same attendant that stopped Holly when she was entering the plane approaches. "You rang?"

"No. I'm fine. Everything's fine. Why?" Holly nervously spouts out.

"I rang," says Nellie. "Can you bring back an extension for the seatbelt?"

He looks Nellie over. "Have you tried extending the one you have as far as it goes? You didn't read to me to be large enough to need an extension," he says.

Nellie takes a deep breath and closes her eyes to find her calm place. Then she looks back to the attendant, who is looking down toward her with what has to be the fakest smile she's seen in a long time. "I'm so glad you read me. I hope you enjoyed it and paid full price. But, I wasn't asking for me. This lady that you are hovering over could use an extension to make her flight more comfortable. You are still interested in having passengers leave happy, aren't you?" she says in a most eloquent, yet forced polite way.

"Ah, yeah sure," he says while barely acknowledging Holly before walking away.

"Thank you. I don't know why I didn't think of asking for one of those," Charley says to Nellie.

"Not a problem. You two look like you deserve a little breather. Rest now, because when the baby comes the sleep will be non-existent for a while. Other than the pregnancy, I don't know what you've been through, but you both look a little weary. No phones are going to ring on this flight. No emails are going to come in that can't wait. Let this plane ride be the gift that gives you rest," she counsels.

On the next row up, Alonya is staring out her newly acquired window. Jacq is now going through her notebook attempting to study her handwritten notes, but all the words are starting to run together. She puts the notebook in the seat pocket in front of her. She takes a moment to look out the window herself. Frank inadvertently turns his head toward her for no particular reason. Their eyes meet. They both look away, but realizing how odd that seems, then both turn back in synchronicity making the exchange even more awkward. Frank chuckles. He extends his hand to her. "I'm Frank Walker by the way. And this is my daughter ..."

"Alonya," Jacq says. "You've got quite the little negotiator there." She shakes his hand. "I'm Jacq Murphy."

Frank's brow scrunches up for a brief second at hearing her name. He tries to cover his reaction, but she didn't miss it. "I'm missing the red hair, freckles, and a few other male parts needed for my name to make sense to you?" she asks.

"No, not at all. I think you're name is lovely," he answers. Then he can't help but ask, "So, was your dad hoping for a boy?"

"That would make for a good story, but no. It's the sales industry that wants a boy. My mom is horrified that I chopped Jacqueline down. But a woman's got to do what a woman's got to do," she says.

"I've met lots of saleswomen through the years. It would have never occurred to me that you'd need to change your name," he says.

"You and my mom have met, I see. Yes, if I was selling women's clothes, I'm sure it would be fine, but I started off in car sales. Got to be tougher than the toughest guy in that world to survive," she explains. She then looks down at her stored notebook, and takes it out. "I should get back to work."

They both start reading their respective books at the same time as the flight attendant returns with Holly's seatbelt extender, and simultaneously as the captain turns on the seatbelt light. "Ah just in time," the attendant says as he hands the extender to her.

Holly studies the extender to see how it works. She looks up to ask the attendant a question only to see that he has already returned to his seat. She looks to Charley. He has his head laid back with his eyes closed. Knowing he was up all night putting this trip together, she decides to leave him alone hoping he'll get some much needed rest. She studies the extender a little more until she sees how the two ends hook into the opposite pieces of the seatbelt. She hooks everything into the proper places and breathes a sigh of relief finally feeling comfortable. That comfort is short lived. "Oh man," she says.

Nellie looks around Charley. "You okay?" she asks.

"It's just now that I'm finally comfortable, I have to go to the bathroom again," Holly explains. "I don't know why I'm having to go so much today. I haven't even had a lot to drink." She unhooks the belt and stands up.

As if in a magic trick, the attendant is suddenly by her side. "I'm sorry. I'm going to have to ask you to sit back down," he says.

"I have to go to the bathroom."

"The captain has turned on the seatbelt sign, which means I need you to take your seat to comply with federal regulations," he insists.

"But I have to go to the bathroom," she says again.

"For security purposes, I need you to follow my instructions," he says sternly.

"Give me a break. Can you not see that the woman is pregnant?" Nellie jumps into the discussion.

"Yes ma'am. I'm fully aware that she's seven months pregnant. And for the safety of her baby, as well as the other passengers, I need her to take her seat. I'm just following regulations," he says.

"Seven months?" Nellie contemplates while staring at Holly's belly.

By this point, Charley is fully awake and is watching the words shoot back and forth ping-pong style until the conversation moves into dangerous territory. "Yes. She's got a couple more months to go before our little one joins the family," he says with a pleading look in his eyes to Nellie.

She gets it. Then she looks back to the attendant. "Please explain to the captain that you've got a pregnant woman whose body is overriding his request for her to be seated."

He says nothing, but doesn't move out of Holly's way either. It seems they've hit a point where he or Holly will have to give into the other. He turns his attention away from Nellie, but she isn't finished just yet. "You can either let this woman use the lavatory or her seat, either way, she's about to relieve herself. And for the sake of her, as well as we fellow passengers, I'm asking you to let her do it there rather than here. If you'd ever had a baby pushing up against your bladder you'd understand that she has little control over this matter," Nellie concludes.

The attendant tries to hold his ground, but realizes he has lost this battle of wills and steps aside. Holly scurries off to the restroom. The attendant sighs and walks the other direction.

Charley turns to Nellie. "Thank you for the second time today. It helped having someone who knows what it's like to be pregnant to talk to that man."

"Oh, I never had a baby. I just saw someone in need of an attitude adjustment," she says. "I'm really good at adjusting attitudes."

Charley's laugh is followed by a sigh. He hangs his head down. He contemplates something. Then, he looks at Nellie, who is staring back with genuine concern.

"When you said I looked weary before … I mean, did you notice anything specific?" he asks.

"Was there something you wanted me to see?"

"No. I was just wondering if, if you … I mean … things are just really tough right now," he finally gets out.

"Well I would first correct you by pointing out that I said the both of you look weary, so you're not in this alone. I can see that you want to be the man that fixes this, whatever this is. Do the two of you know what it is? Have you discussed it?" she asks.

"I guess with the baby coming …" he gets out before Nellie interrupts.

"No, you can't blame it on the baby. Nor can you expect that a baby is going to fix it. The baby will bring you joy, if you are free to truly experience his or her innocence, but … well, you asked me what I saw. You look sad. And she looks mad. Sweet, but mad. Don't get me wrong; people think I'm mad about stuff sometimes too. I dare say our friend the flight attendant might describe me that way. So I'm not saying mad is bad," she adds with a laugh. He smiles, enjoying her company. For no apparent reason, he feels a freedom to be open to this here-to-fore stranger. But the light moment is quickly filled with another sigh.

"Are you sad about what she's mad about?" she asks.

"Yeah, I think so. But I don't know what to do to make it better," he says. "We made this move to Phoenix because of my work. It was one of those offers that you just had to take. I mean, I'm just a repo man, but a neighbor from where I grew up, he helped me get the job. He's helped several guys from the neighborhood get jobs with the bank. And he said that in order to really work my way up, I'd have to be willing to move around for a while to wherever the bank wanted me to go. And it wasn't just me. Holly was excited about the chance to go see other parts of the country too ... until we got there. Then she realized that seeing other parts of the country meant not seeing her momma every day, or any of her friends. And I didn't know what to do. I still don't know what to do. I've done everything I could think of to make her happy, but she's just homesick. And as hard as I try, I can't make up for all the people she's missing. So that's why we're taking this last minute trip home for Christmas. But ..." He's interrupted again, but this time by Holly's return.

She is all smiles as she puts her hand on his shoulder to help lower herself into the seat. "I feel better now. What are you two talking about?" she asks.

He turns away from Nellie. "Nothing. Just how happy we are to be going home for Christmas," he says with a pat to Holly's leg. Realizing she can't fix it for him, Nellie looks out the window.

* * * * * * *

Later, Nellie is humming while looking out the window. Charley and Holly are watching the airline's movie selection. In row 17, Frank and Alonya are also watching the film, while Jacq remains hard at work on her laptop.

The movie ends and the four viewers remove their headsets. Alonya promptly raises her window shade. She stares out the window for a few minutes until she tunes in on Nellie's humming. She stands in her seat looking back to row 18. "Are you a singer?" she asks Nellie.

"Why, yes I am. Are you a singer?" Nellie asks.

"Nah. I used to sing with my mom though," Alonya answers.

"But you don't anymore?" Nellie inquires.

Frank tries to pull Alonya down into her seat, but she pulls back to continue talking to her new friend. "Alonya, stop bothering her," he says.

"She's not bothering me. This is a long flight for someone her age. I understand that. Really, it's a long flight for someone my age, too. She's fine," Nellie tells Frank. She then looks back to Alonya, who is still focused on her.

"Now, why don't you sing with your mother anymore?" Nellie asks.

"She died," Alonya answers.

"I see." Out of the many things this little girl could've said, that wasn't on the list of expected responses. "Well, I guess she's singing with the angels now," she finally replies.

Alonya smiles. "That's what my dad says."

"He's a wise man. You're blessed to have him. Would you like to sing with me?" Nellie asks her new friend.

"That's okay. You sounded good like you were doing it," Alonya says.

Holly has been listening to this conversation of young and old. "Awww, I hope my baby grows up to be as sweet as you," she says.

"I don't know," Alonya says with a twinkle in her eye. "My dad says I'm one of a kind."

"And he is absolutely correct about that," Nellie concurs.

Holly unhooks her seatbelt, and pushes herself up out of the seat. "Back to the bathroom," she says.

"You okay?" Charley asks.

"Yeah, everything's fine," she responds as she walks away.

On row 17, Jacq has tried to continue working, but has mostly been listening to Alonya's chat with Nellie. She leans over to Frank. "That's quite a little charmer you have," she says.

"She's definitely an independent spirit," he responds.

Jacq stops the façade of working by pushing her laptop back. She turns to Frank for genuine conversation. "Alonya is an original name. Where does it come from?" she inquires.

"Both of her grandfathers – kind of. My dad's name is John, and Rosa's, that's her mother, Rosa's father's name was Juan. We wanted to call her Lon, which rhymed with both of their names, but that didn't feel like a real name. So, we named her Alonya thinking Lon could be her nickname. But then, Lon was quickly becoming Lonnie, and while I loved Lonnie Anderson when I was a kid, I didn't want that to become my daughter's name. So, we started calling her by her full name, which was built around what we thought her nickname would be," he finishes the complicated explanation. "I should just tell people she's named after a relative. It would be simpler."

Jacq looks down and shifts into panic mode. "Oh no. No. Please don't do this," she exclaims.

Frank looks around quickly to figure out if he did something, or what might be happening, but sees nothing. "What's wrong?" he asks wanting to help her, both genuinely and because people are starting to stare.

"What's wrong, Daddy?" Alonya asks.

He puts his arm around his little girl and gives her a reassuring pat on the arm. "I'm not sure, but it'll be okay. Just read your book right now." He takes a children's book out of the seat pocket in front of Alonya. She takes the book timidly and opens it. Looking out of the corner of her eye, she sees that her dad has turned his attention back to the screaming lady. Alonya closes her book and watches the drama that's unfolding.

"You cannot do this to me," Jacq almost yells as she hits the side of her laptop.

Frank relaxes when he sees it's just a computer problem. "Wait," he says while reaching to take her laptop from her. "That's not going to fix anything. What's happened?"

She firms up her grip on the computer. "It's crashed. My whole presentation just disappeared. I don't have enough time to redo all that work," she explains having started to tear up. "It took me about eighteen hours to assimilate all of that data."

Frank attempts a second time to take the computer. Her grip is still strong as she stares helplessly at the blank screen. Frank slowly releases his grip. "I'm the guy you would call if you were in your office. I work in I.T.," he says softly hoping to ease her tension. Her face eases from panic to only slightly distressed. She passes the laptop over to him.

"I'm assuming that nothing is backed up?" he asks.

"Some things are ... I think. Doesn't it back up automatically?" she answers as the stress starts to build back up. "Can you save my presentation?"

He doesn't answer, but shrugs his shoulders as he begins checking the normal problem areas. The screen lights back up. Frank types in some standard codes, and like magic Jacq's presentation reappears on the screen. "Okay, is this where you were?" he asks, feeling a little like a superhero.

Jacq grabs the computer from his lap, almost hugging it. "You just saved my life. Seriously, I can't begin to think of how to repay you."

"I take it you're not flying toward a vacation like the rest of us?"

She shakes her head. "I'm pitching a new client in New York an hour after the plane lands."

"That's cutting it close. Good thing we took off on time," he says with no response from Jacq, who is busy going page by page through her PowerPoint presentation. "Working on Christmas Eve? Must be really important work. Do you at least have family in the area to celebrate with tonight?" he asks trying to make conversation.

"I'll be back in Phoenix tonight," she answers while remaining focused on her work.

"What's the important pitch?" he asks.

Jacq stops scanning through her files. She contemplates how to make it sound more important before admitting, "Spa packages."

"Spa packages?" he repeats while questioning if he heard her correctly. She nods. "That couldn't wait until after the holidays?" he asks.

"An old client we've been trying to get new business out of called yesterday. He said today was the only day he was available to spend his end of the year money," she explains.

Frank starts to chuckle. The chuckle builds into a snicker, which builds into a laugh. Jacq begins to find his reaction insulting. She turns away from him, but can't focus on her work. As he settles down, he says, "I'm sorry. You'd have to have been in my head the last week or so to understand," he says.

"Try me," she retorts with no humor on her face.

He loses the last of his laugh as he realizes she is not entertained by his response. "It's just that, well, you're a

45

workaholic. And your job is to convince others to take time off to relax," he says.

"You're not the first to point out the irony that's my life," she says. "But what does that have to do with ..."

"Is that the presentation?" he interrupts.

"Yes," she responds. "Why?"

"Nothing," he says unconvincingly. "It's just that ... Sorry. The geek comes out in me with this stuff. I'm an I.T. guy, but I've just finished all my courses in graphic design," he answers.

"And you see something wrong with my presentation?" she asks.

"Not wrong, just not as good as it could be if you're planning to project it. If you're going to be working straight off your computer, it's fine," he says.

Jacq is suddenly experiencing a mixture of insult and intrigue. "I'm going to project it," she says. "Are you saying you can make it better?"

"I could do a couple of things in the programming that would make your pictures really pop out more," he says.

They stare at one another without speaking for a moment. Jacq is the first to break. She hands the computer back over to him. "And you can do this without crashing the computer again?" she asks.

"Um, correction. It crashed under your control. I brought it back to life. But yes, I'll save your file as it is, and make a copy of it that I'll work on in a new file," he explains as he begins typing.

Jacq breathes easy, perhaps for the first time since take off. "Who are you and the lovely Alonya visiting in New York?" she asks.

Alonya, who has continued to watch this whole exchange between her dad and Jacq, jumps in. "We're going to see my grandparents in Washington D.C. My papa works for Congress," she adds.

"Wow. That's pretty cool," Jacq says turning her attention from Frank to Alonya.

"My dad's a security guard at the Capitol building. Don't let her mislead you," he says cutting his eye to Alonya.

"She's good. She used the facts to tell the story she wanted to tell," Jacq says.

"All while selling you a completely different package than the one you were looking at," he responds. Then it hits him, "I guess you, being in sales, would see that as more positive than most, including her father."

"Is it too early to sign her to an exclusive contract?" she asks with a laugh. Frank joins her in a light chuckle until they both peter off, but continue looking at one another.

Alonya, who is clueless to the flirtatious moment that's in progress, leans around her dad to speak to Jacq. "I'm only two degrees away from the President of the United States."

47

Frank and Jacq break out of their shared moment. Jacq looks to Alonya, while still lingering on what just happened with Frank. "Two degrees?" she asks.

"Yeah, because everyone's only six degrees away from anyone else. That's what my papa told me. Well, he shook hands with the President. So that makes me two degrees away from the White House, and only three degrees away from pretty much every other person in charge of running the world," Alonya explains with a smile. "And, now you're only three and four degrees away from all those people because you met us."

"How lucky I am to have met you," Jacq says impressed with Alonya's depth of thought on the subject. She and Frank share another quick flirtatious glance before she goes back to reading through her notebook.

In the lavatory, Holly washes her hands in the cramped, tiny space. While steadying herself with one hand, she uses the other to pull out a few paper towels. With a bit of rocking back and forth, she manages to get both hands dry without having to sit or fall down. Just as she unlocks the door to exit, a pain strikes horizontally across her stomach. She's gotten used to pings of pain, but this is different and lasting. She grips the handrail to steady herself. The pain finally fades away. She takes a moment. A few deep breaths with a hand resting on her belly seems to get things back to normal. Without saying anything, she looks at herself in the mirror. That was scary. She takes one more deep breath, shakes it off, and pulls the door open. As she makes her way back up the aisle, a bell dings and the seatbelt light turns on. She gets to her row. "I saw the seatbelt sign come on. Are we about to land?" she asks.

"Yep. Good thing you made it back before that flight attendant saw you. We don't want to have to call Nellie back into action," he says. Nellie acknowledges his comment with a smile and then glances back out the window.

Holly maneuvers her stomach between the back of Jacq's seat and the armrest of her own in order to sit down. "I am ready to get off this plane," she says, slightly out of breath.

"We have a quick layover, so we'll have to hurry to the next gate. As soon as they open the door, go ahead and get off. I'll grab our bags and catch up," he says.

She nods before laying her head back, and closing her eyes.

Chapter 4

The passengers from the Phoenix flight enter Newark Liberty International Airport. Jacq, Frank, and Alonya stop in the concourse. "I guess this is goodbye. Have a great time in Washington," Jacq says.

Frank is mesmerized looking at her and then realizes there is a silent moment awaiting his response. "Ah, yeah. Good luck with your pitch," he replies. "Enjoy what you can of New York. I know you said you'll be rushing in and out, but it's one of the best cities to be in this time of year."

Alonya spontaneously hugs Jacq. "Merry Christmas," says Alonya.

Surprised by the unexpected contact, Jacq stands still for a moment before responding. She finally leans over giving Alonya a pat on the back hug adding, "You too." She then pulls herself back into her sales persona. "I'm sure that hug will bring me extra luck today. Got to rush off so I can make my meeting."

Jacq speeds away. Frank reaches out to her saying, "It was great meeting you too." But Jacq is not likely to have heard him, as she disappears into the crowd. They walk away.

As Frank and Alonya drift off into the crowd of travelers, Holly walks through the door with Nellie. "Thank you again for helping get me to the bathroom," says Holly.

"You're welcome, baby." Holly winces. She puts her hand on her belly. Nellie reaches out to her. "Are you okay?" she asks.

Charley enters the terminal with their carry-on bags in time to see this. He rushes up to Holly. "What's wrong?" he gasps.

The pain has passed. Holly straightens up insisting that she's okay. "Nothing's wrong. The little one's just hopping up and down on the bladder today. Let's find me a bathroom," she says.

Charley's stress shows as his eyes bulge and he lets out an exacerbated breath. "We've got to hurry to catch our next plane. Can you wait?" he urges.

Nellie looks at him with every bit of attitude she gave to the flight attendant earlier as she clears her throat. "You remember what I told that man on the plane? That goes for you too."

Holly looks at him with pouty eyes and a big smile. "I'll be quick," she says.

He knows that this isn't a negotiation, so Charley nods his head. He takes his cell phone out of his coat pocket and turns it on. No sooner is it powered up before it starts chiming with voicemail and text alerts. He looks down at the phone. A text on the screen reads: *Call Work. NOW.*

Holly starts to look at his phone, but he puts it away before she can read the text. "Who'd you get a text from?" she asks.

"Nobody, just a stupid sales pitch. Come on. Let's get you to the bathroom before Nellie whoops me," he says.

Holly hugs Nellie. "You sure you're okay?" Nellie asks.

"Yes ma'am. Thank you again," Holly says.

Charley reaches over and hugs Nellie as well. "It was a real pleasure meeting you. Merry Christmas," he adds.

"Merry Christmas. Get that baby to Arkansas safely," she says.

Charley and Holly walk off. The electric cart arrives to take Nellie to her next gate. Before getting on, she can't help but look back at the young couple with some concern.

* * * * * * *

Frank and Alonya walk toward their next departure gate. They each have a large fountain soda. Frank is also carrying a grease-stained brown paper bag. Suddenly Alonya takes off running. "Alonya!" he calls out to stop her. Then he sees Nellie sitting in the waiting area ahead. He smiles admiring how easy it is for his daughter to make new friends. He follows her lead rather than giving a second attempt at calling her back to him.

"It's the singing lady," she says as she arrives in front of Nellie.

"She has a name. Introduce yourself," Frank suggests with a smile to Nellie.

Alonya passes her drink off to her dad. She extends her hand to Nellie. "Hi. I'm Alonya Walker. What's your name?"

Nellie smiles ear to ear. She takes Alonya's hand. "Hello Alonya Walker. It's very nice to meet you. My name is Nellie Goldman," she answers.

Alonya points back at Frank. "That's Daddy," she explains.

Frank tucks the food bag and two drinks between his left arm and chest, while extending his right hand to Nellie. "Hi. I'm Frank," he says. Nellie shakes his hand too.

Alonya hops into the empty seat next to Nellie. "Are you going to Washington D.C. too?" she asks.

"No. I'm going to my sister's in Detroit. It looks like my plane leaves from the gate next to yours," she answers.

There is another empty seat on the other side of Alonya. Frank hands Alonya her drink and the bag of food as he parks the luggage to the side of that seat. "Do you mind if we join you?" he asks.

"Good company is always welcomed," Nellie replies.

Before handing the food bag to her dad, Alonya takes out a cheeseburger that is so large it requires her to use both hands. Nellie watches curiously as this little girl maneuvers such a big burger. Alonya opens her mouth as wide as it will go and then chomps down. As she chews and chews on her mouthful, Nellie looks down at the burger that Alonya has placed on its wrapper in her lap. The after effect of all this effort is only the appearance of a nibble.

"They didn't have a child's size?" Nellie asks.

Alonya holds up a finger to indicate she needs a moment to finish chewing. She chews a little more, and a little more until finally she swallows. "This is my Christmas Eve burger. It's supposed to be big," she explains.

"I've heard of a lot of things, but I've never heard of a Christmas Eve burger," Nellie responds.

"That's because it's mine and Daddy's own special Christmas tradition."

Nellie looks at Frank, who is chewing a mouthful of burger himself. It doesn't take him as long to chew and swallow before he can explain. "For the last couple of years, we've flown to my parents in Washington D.C. Like today, we pretty much always end up with a connection instead of a direct flight. A couple of years ago, we were in an airport where the only thing we could find to eat was fast food, and they were out of the kid packs. Since then, we've made it our tradition that she and I get one big messy burger each as part of our Christmas travels," he says.

"Mommy used to get one too, but she always said it wasn't good for us," Alonya adds.

"And you eat that whole burger?" Nellie asks Alonya.

"Nope, but one day when I'm big I will," she says confidently.

With great appreciation for the effort, Nellie says, "Yes you will baby. Yes you will."

* * * * * * *

In the ladies room, Holly comes out of a stall. She goes to a sink and washes her hands. Mid-wash, a pain strikes her stomach again. She reacts by pulling her hand from the sink onto her pregnant belly. The pain subsides. Like before, she takes a moment to shake off the fear of what just happened, then turns off the sink, and dries her hands. A look in the mirror reveals a wet handprint on her shirt centered on her baby bump. She brushes it off as best she can and walks out of the bathroom.

Charley is waiting in the corridor, as patiently as one can when they feel they should be rushing. He hands Holly her coat and purse when she comes out. "We need to walk as fast as you can, okay?" he says. He turns to start walking, but does a double take when he notices her shirt. "Why is there a handprint on your shirt? Is everything okay?"

She walks past him looking back to say, "Everything's fine. Come on. I thought we had to hurry."

Charley and Holly approach their gate. Two frazzled desk clerks attempt to organize the paperwork from the flight that just departed. Charley points out a nearby empty seat, but Holly wants to make sure she gets an aisle seat for the second leg.

Finally as one of the clerks walks away, the other acknowledges the young couple. "May I help you?" she asks. Charley hands her their boarding passes. She looks them over, then looks up with a deadpan emotionless face and says, "We closed this flight out fifteen minutes ago."

"No," Holly exclaims.

"You've got to get us on. We'll be quick," Charley begs.

Feeling the couple's desperation, the clerk softens. "I would if I could, but the plane just took off. You're really late," she explains.

Holly starts to cry. "I shouldn't have gone to the bathroom," she says.

Charley takes her in his arms. "Don't blame yourself. You weren't in there fifteen minutes," he says to comfort her.

"No," the clerk agrees. "Your flight from Phoenix arrived late. They didn't tell you?"

"Not a word," Charley says. "I thought we left on time. When is the next flight?"

The clerk scans the crowded airport behind them. "Let me see what I can do. We have people that have been here for two days trying to get out," she explains.

Holly's hands instinctually reach for her belly. "Two days? I can't wait that long," she exclaims. Picking up the panic in her voice, Charley and the clerk look at Holly with concern. She attempts to cover her outburst. "We'll have missed Christmas by then."

The clerk begins typing on her computer. She searches through the data looking for something that will work. "Okay," she says as she starts typing again. "If anyone asks, you were extremely upset and on the acceptable side of rude with me."

Holly reacts. "We didn't mean to be rude. We just ..."

"That's just what I'm saying so that I can give you these two sets of first class tickets to get you home," the clerk interjects.

"First class?" Holly relaxes. "Oh, thank you."

Charley runs this exchange of words back through his head. "Did you say two sets?" he asks.

"Yes. Sorry to say, the only way I can get you to Little Rock tonight is to send you to Washington D.C. first," she admits as she continues typing.

* * * * * * *

Back at the D.C. gate, Alonya has her princess bag of stuffed animals opened and halfway unpacked. She holds up an old stuffed lavender elephant that is faded and droopy. "This is EE the Elephant. I sleep with him every night," she proudly announces to Nellie.

"He looks like you've been sleeping with him for a long time," Nellie replies.

Alonya hugs EE affectionately. "I've had him my whole life," she says.

"He was a gift from her uncle when she was born," Frank adds.

Charley and Holly approach the gate. Alonya is the first to spot them. "It's the pregnant lady!" she exclaims.

Alonya's voice draws their attention. Holly's face brightens. Charley smiles when he sees Nellie.

"Is your gate over here too?" Nellie asks. "I didn't notice anything going to Arkansas."

"We missed our flight," Charley explains.

"Oh," Nellie says with a twinge of concern.

"But a really nice woman found us a way home. We just have to fly to Washington D.C. first," Holly adds.

An odd vibration comes through the speakers followed by, "Ladies and gentlemen. Flight 174 to Washington D.C. is being delayed due to a blizzard that has hit the Carolinas. Please don't crowd the desk. We will give you more information as soon as we get it."

Frank and Charley immediately hang their heads low hearing this news. Holly looks somewhat confused. "What does that mean?" she asks.

"It means we'll be here a little longer than expected, but we'll be okay," Charley says to comfort her. His cell phone rings. He reaches in his pants pocket and turns it off without taking it out. "Let's see if we can find somewhere for you to sit down," he suggests.

"You're not going to answer your phone? What if it's Momma calling to check on us?" Holly suggests.

"When has your mom ever dialed my number? Besides she doesn't even know we're coming. Since I booked our flight in the middle of the night, I couldn't call anyone."

"Who's going to pick us up if nobody knows we're coming?" Holly says more so than asks.

"Let's get there first," he says. Charley scans the crowded terminal looking for empty seats.

Nellie leans over to Alonya. "Miss Holly needs a place to sit to keep the baby rested. Do you think she could have your seat?"

"Sure," Alonya says. She hops onto the floor among her stuffed pals with no hesitation.

"Oh you are so sweet," Holly says as she gladly sits down. She shuffles around a bit shifting her coat, purse, and body until she finds the right spot. She realizes Charley is still standing. "Where are you going to sit?" she asks with concern.

"I'm good," he says. "Something will open up, or I bet Alonya there will let me join her party."

Alonya doesn't hear him as she's busy having playtime with EE and a pink rabbit. Frank chuckles. "There's always room for another as long as you like imaginary tea," he says.

"Imaginary is my favorite kind of tea," he replies.

Holly looks from Alonya to Charley. "Did you ever look to see who was calling you?" she asks.

"Um," he searches for an explanation hoping he had already dodged this conversation.

Suddenly the vibration comes from the speakers again followed by, "Ladies and gentlemen, we are now announcing the delay of Flight 227 to Detroit. We will give you more information as soon as it becomes available."

"Wonder what that's about? Detroit can handle snow. I wouldn't think it would be affected by that blizzard because it isn't anywhere near the Carolinas," Nellie says.

"Do you want me to go check for you?" Charley eagerly offers.

"Would you? That would be lovely," she responds.

Charley nods and takes off. As soon as he is out of sight of Holly, he stops. He reaches into his pocket and takes his phone out. The screen indicates he had five waiting messages. He hits a button and holds the phone up to his ear.

The computer voice politely says, "Message one." That is followed by the jovial voice of his boss, Steve. "Hey Charley. We haven't heard from you this morning. Just calling to see how close you are."

"Message two," the voicemail voice calls out. Followed by Steve saying, "Charley. Still haven't heard from you. I know it's Christmas Eve and all, but the sooner we get the work done, the sooner we can all enjoy the holiday."

"Message three." "Dude what are you doing? The longer you take to get here, the longer we all have to stay. This is not like you. Call me as soon as you get this."

"Message four." "You have exactly fifteen minutes to call me or your Christmas gift will be exchanged for a nice, new, shiny termination."

"Message five." "Merry Christmas. You're fired."

Charley nods his head in agreement as he hears the last message. It would have been more shocking if his boss had let him off the hook. He puts his phone back in his pocket and starts walking back toward the group. He makes it almost all the way back when he remembers his original task was to find out about Nellie's flight.

He turns back before anyone sees him. The Detroit gate has at least twenty people waiting in line. Charley is starting to feel like nothing is going his way. Then the odd vibration rings through the speakers followed by: "Ladies and gentlemen. Yes, we know that Detroit isn't near the Carolinas. However, the plane meant to take you to Detroit is coming from Charlotte, NC. We are currently waiting to see if that plane can take off. If not, the airline is working on getting another plane here to get you on your way. Again, please don't crowd the desk. We will announce more information as soon as it becomes available."

Charley heads back. On his short walk, Steve's voice keeps playing over and over on a loop in his head. *"Merry Christmas. You're fired." "Merry Christmas. You're fired." "Merry Christmas. You're fired."* By the time he arrives back to the group, he is in agony wondering what he's done. He is not only responsible to support himself and Holly, but there's a new baby due any day now. That job was supposed to have him on the right path of financial stability for years to come. And on a whim in the middle of the night, he blew it. Suddenly he finds himself completely on the other side of the country, hanging out in an airport with a group of people he just met, with a future so uncertain it's not even clear where he'll be sleeping tonight.

He tries to pull himself together by focusing on giving Nellie the information about her flight. Now is not the time to share the news with Holly. He'll let her get home, enjoy Christmas like she wants to, then find a way to tell her before the baby comes. He'll keep the secret a few days at best. But before he can even open his mouth, Nellie thanks him for trying, but says that she was able to hear the announcement.

Holly detects his stress level. "What's wrong?" she asks.

"Nothing," he says.

"I can see it on your face. Something's bothering you. What is it?" she insists.

He looks around to avoid direct eye contact with his wife who knows him all too well. A restroom sign catches his attention. "I just need to go to the men's room. I'll be back in a minute," he says as he dashes off.

"I should call my sister," Nellie says as she reaches into her purse. She digs around shifting the contents from one side to the other. "I know I have a phone card in here somewhere."

Frank reaches into the inside pocket of his jacket and pulls out his cell phone. He extends it to her. "You can use my cell if you'd like."

"Oh that is so nice of you. Are you sure it won't cost you anything? I'm calling Detroit," she says.

"Unless Detroit has moved out of the country, it'll be fine. I have plenty of minutes left," he assures her.

Nellie takes the phone. She tentatively dials the number, and then stares at the keypad before pushing the "Talk" button.

In Detroit, the phone in Opal's kitchen rings. In a similar pace to Nellie the night before, Opal slowly makes her way toward the phone. Upon getting there, she reaches over to a nearby shelf and picks up a pair of reading glasses. The phone continues to ring as she puts on glasses to read the caller I.D. She then picks up the phone receiver with a little extra attitude. "I can't say I know a Frank Walker. Do you know me? Or are you trying to sell me something on Christmas Eve?" she says in lieu of a simple hello.

"What are you talking about?" Nellie asks.

"Nellie, is that you?" Opal asks.

"Yes," she responds. "What were you going on about somebody selling you something?"

"People try to sell you stuff every day of the year nowadays. My caller I.D. says someone else is calling. Where are you?" Opal inquires further.

"I'm calling to tell you I'm stuck in Newark. They're not sure when we'll be in Detroit because of a snowstorm in North Carolina," Nellie explains.

"That doesn't even make sense. How does a storm in a part of the country that you are neither flying to or from affect you getting here? You sure you aren't calling me from this Frank Walker's house? It is a Phoenix number now that I look at it," Opal suggests.

Nellie looks around. Her temper is flaring in a way only her sister can inspire, but Nellie works to stay calm. She clears her throat and smiles at Frank before looking down at the floor. "Opal, I am in the Newark Liberty International Airport. The plane meant to take me from here to there is currently stuck in Charlotte, NC due to a storm. They've said they are working on either getting that plane out of the storm or finding another plane to get us where we need to go. I'll try to call you when we're boarding, but Phillip should call the airline before he goes to pick me up. Now I don't want to use too many minutes on Mr. Walker's phone ... that he was kind enough to let me use. So I'm going to hang up now," Nellie concludes.

"That's who Frank Walker is?" Opal asks with a sudden brightness in her tone. "Did you meet him there at the airport and he just let you use his phone? Is he a nice looking older gentleman interested in making you Nellie Walker? Or did he recognize you from days gone by?"

"I don't need a day that's gone by to be recognized, thank you very much," Nellie scolds her sister.

"So he didn't recognize you then?" Opal assumes.

"Mr. Walker is a very nice young man, who has a seven-year-old daughter named Alonya. They sat in front of me on the first flight. I am going to hang up now so not to over use his generosity," Nellie says ending the conversation.

"Are you okay? Got a warm enough coat? I bet they'd let you in one of those airline clubs with the nicer seats if you asked them. Just sing 'em something," Opal suggests.

"Goodbye sister," Nellie says before pushing the "End" button on Frank's phone. She hands the phone back to Frank. "And now we wait," she says with a bit of a forced smile.

Chapter 5

It's a cold gray day in Manhattan as a black town car pulls in front of a building at 60th Street and Park Avenue. The driver gets out of the car, and comes around to the back passenger door. He opens the door and Jacq gets out. "You'll be back in an hour and a half exactly. Yes?" she confirms.

"You bet. I will be parked here as though I never left," he assures her.

Jacq tips him and then enters the building. Inside, she stops at the directory to double check the floor number. It's the 11th floor, just as her notes indicate. An elevator is already waiting with the door open. She gets on and presses button number "11."

Upstairs, Jacq walks off the elevator and approaches the reception desk. There is no one there. She waits somewhat patiently for a moment. According to the clock on the desk, she is exactly on time – which is ten minutes late for her. This makes her antsy. She decides to go back to find someone. She goes to the only door in the lobby. It is a solid metal door painted brown to blend in with the walls of the room. It's locked.

She decides to look for the button to buzz open the door. It is in the expected place, attached to the bottom of the reception desk to the right side of the chair. Jacq presses the button. "Eeeerp," a sound comes from the door. Satisfied, Jacq walks back over. She pulls on the handle. It's still locked. Seems that no buzz equals no opening door. She goes back to the desk to study the possibilities. Can she press the button and get back to the door before the buzz stops? She tries it. Button pressed, "Eeeerp," run to the door. Locked. Three more times she tries it, each time getting a little closer, but never close enough. One more try, she decides. With one hand stretching toward the door, she gets into a weird yoga-like pose to reach her other hand the opposite direction. She's feeling pretty good about this attempt. "Eeee ...." Her finger makes contact with the button. She stretches even closer toward the door, but still has her eyes on the button. Determined that the turn and leap will need to happen simultaneously for success, she prepares herself. "One, two, three!" She turns and leaps – right onto a 200-pound black woman with Chaka Khan-like big hair.

The woman screams. Jacq screams. They both slam against the door. Jacq has hit her intended target in an unintentional way. She quickly pushes off the woman. "I am so sorry. Where did you come from?" she asks.

The woman brushes herself off with a slight growl as she looks up toward Jacq. "What were you doing?"

"I asked you a question first," Jacq suggests.

The woman crosses her arms saying nothing but clearly stating that her question is the only one she cares about. Jacq gives in. "I was trying to get into the offices. I have an appointment, but the receptionist isn't here. She ... or he must have holiday-itis. Right? Too busy celebrating to work. There's two of us needing assistance, and no receptionist to be found," Jacq adds trying to win the woman over to her side.

"Can I help you?" the woman asks with her arms still crossed.

Jacq freezes as the realization washes over her. "You're the receptionist?"

The woman doesn't reply, but the answer is evident. "I thought maybe you were on break so I ... uh ...," she fades off. She takes a breath. "Hi, I'm here for a meeting with Robert Macina."

"I don't think he's in today," she replies.

Jacq's mouth drops open in shock. "That's not possible. He set this meeting up yesterday, saying that it had to be today."

The receptionist stares at Jacq without saying anything for another moment. Finally she says, "If you'd like to step around to your side of the desk, I'll check with his office."

"Oh," Jacq looks around realizing that she's still standing in front of the receptionist's seat. "Right. Let me just ...," she stops speaking and quickly moves around to the front of the desk.

The receptionist claims her territory by plopping down into her seat. She puts on her headset and dials an extension number.

"Hey. There's a lady in the lobby saying she has an appointment with Robert," she tells Mr. Macina's assistant. "I already told her that. She says that Robert set it up yesterday. He told her it had to be today." There's another pause as she listens to the assistant's response. "I don't know," she says incredulously before looking up toward Jacq. "Are you the spa lady?"

"Yes," Jacq answers hoping this recognition is a good sign.

"Yep," the receptionist says into the phone. After another short pause she says, "Either way, she's here." She hits a button disconnecting the call and looks back up to Jacq. "His assistant is coming out to see you."

Jacq starts to pace as she waits for the inevitable bad news. The assistant tentatively enters the lobby. "Hi. You're Ms. Murphy?" she asks.

As though the assistant was the decision maker for the sale Jacq was hoping to make today, she grabs the assistant's hand. "Jacq. And you're ...?"

"Brenda. I'm Mr. Macina's assistant," she responds while seeming to hold her breath as she prepares to give the bad news. "I'm really sorry about the mix up. He isn't here today," she finally gets out.

A little less deflated hearing the news for the second time, Jacq asks, "How is that possible? He called my office yesterday insisting that we have a meeting today."

"Right. Then his wife gave him an earful about having a meeting about vacation packages when he was supposed to be on holiday himself. He told me he was calling you back," she explains.

"I flew in from Phoenix for this meeting," Jacq says.

"No you didn't. That is just wrong," the receptionist interjects.

The assistant cuts a look to her co-worker sending the message to "shut it." She re-gathers her comforting smile and turns back to Jacq. "I don't know what to say," she says. "I'm sure this will be a great bargaining chip when you finally have the meeting."

"He's definitely going to owe you," the receptionist chimes in.

The assistant clears her throat and holds her hand up toward the receptionist, while maintaining a frozen smile for Jacq. "Hopefully this will turn into a great opportunity to experience Christmas in New York before you go back to Arizona. I wish I could do more. Can I have Kim get your overcoat?" she offers.

"I … I don't have one," Jacq responds.

"Okay then," the assistant says with a nod. "Well, I'll have Mr. Macina call you after the holidays to set something up." She shakes Jacq's hand and quickly slips back into the locked office area.

"Unbelievable," Jacq says as she watches the door close.

"You got some friends to visit at least?" the receptionist asks.

Jacq turns and walks out without responding.

Back down in the lobby, she paces back and forth holding her cell phone to her ear. "I know what I scheduled. Is there any way he can come back now?" she says with some insistence in her tone. There is a pause as she listens to the response. Then she says, "I'm sure it is, but I'm not interested in the city's decorations. You know what? Tell him to forget it. Cancel the return trip. I'll catch a cab," she says with determination before disconnecting the call.

She walks outside and throws her hand up. The cold air sets in as five taxicabs drive pass one by one. Frustrated, she stops a man walking by. "Is there a better way to catch a cab to the airport?" she asks.

"In this weather on Christmas Eve? Good luck," he says with true New Yorker sarcasm. "The subway is your best bet."

"Fine. Which one will take me to Newark?" Jacq asks for further direction.

"You're going to Newark? Yeah, you're screwed. You need to catch the shuttle from Port Authority," he instructs. "From here, you'll want to catch the N or the R. It's a little bit of a walk in no more than you're wearing. You need a coat," he recommends.

"I don't have one. So what's the fastest way to get to the N or the R subway station?" she asks starting to lose her patience.

"Well, if you were dressed right to be in New York during the winter, I'd tell you to walk down 5th Avenue. That's two avenue blocks, though. With no coat and in those shoes, you'd hate yourself before you got there. There's nothing like this city and that avenue at Christmas time, though. All the decorations, and department store windows ..."

Jacq cuts him off. "Why does everyone keep trying to cram Christmas in this city down my throat? And I'm dressed perfectly to do everything that I was supposed to do today. Now, where is the subway station that will get me out of here as fast as possible?" she asks, ending her blowup.

The man throws his hands up in the air as he starts walking away. "Find it yourself if you don't want to hear what I have to say."

"No. Wait," she begs. But he disappears in the crowd. She stops an older lady, who is bundled up in a sleeping bag style down coat with a hood. "Excuse me. Can you tell me where the N or the R subway station is that will take me to Port Authority?" Jacq asks with far more humility this time.

The lady looks at Jacq from head to toe before speaking. "One short block, and one long block," the lady says while looking down at Jacq's feet and working her way back up to make eye contact. Jacq looks around still not knowing which direction to walk. "You want to go to 59th and Lex. Walk one short block down to 59th. Turn. Then walk one long block to Lexington Avenue," the lady adds before she starts walking again. She stops and turns back around. "Bloomingdale's is at that corner. You should go in and buy a coat and some sensible shoes." The lady turns away and continues toward her destination.

Jacq realizes after the lady has gone that she still doesn't know which direction to go toward 59th Street. And, the lady said to turn and walk the long block to Lexington, but she didn't say which way to turn. Jacq starts walking briskly down the street to catch up to the woman for that last piece of information. She comes to an intersection as the light is changing from yellow to red, but races across before the traffic starts moving. This bundled up little old lady is proving to be a challenge to catch up to. By the time Jacq reaches the next intersection, the light has already turned red. Through the moving traffic across the street, she sees the woman's coat continue to move further away. In utter frustration, Jacq looks up as if ready to scream at the gods for what her day has turned into. Her mood shifts quickly when she spots the street sign above her. "58th Street." Finally, something has gone right. She's gone one street too far, but the short block was easy enough. She decides she'll get the long block over with, and then back track the short block back to 59th. A sense of confidence refills her. Now, the next direction was to turn. But which way? Jacq looks to her left and then to her right. "All is right in the world again. I think I'll go right," she says to herself.

The breeze picks up as she walks this long block. Jacq tilts her head down to avoid the cold air blowing in her face. The walk has a deceivingly slight uphill slant, so her feet in heels are starting to ache. She pushes through knowing that at the end of this block, she'll reach the subway station … and Bloomingdale's. Maybe she will run in to buy a pair of shoes, she thinks. No need for a coat, because she's about to go underground and then fly back to her warm homeland of Arizona.

Finally, she reaches the next intersection. She looks around confused. This isn't what she was expecting. An inspection of all four corners reveals no subway station, nor any signs that say Bloomingdale's. Jacq looks up to inspect the street signs. One reads 58th Street, and the other says Madison Avenue. She's come the wrong way. Right was wrong. Left was right. To turn around would mean walking not only the treacherous trek that she just completed, but double that because she would then still have to walk the long block she meant to walk in the first place. That's when the first man's advice rings in her head.

"I'd tell you to walk down 5th Avenue. That's two avenue blocks, though," his voice echoes. She looks down at her feet, which are giving her an odd mixture of pounding pain and numbness. Looking back up at the street sign, she realizes at this point she can either finish the two block walk he was suggesting, or start a whole new two block, plus the added short block back that she has to backtrack because of her first mistake. It seems best to keep moving toward 5th, and so she does.

After another torturous block of the continued slightly up hill trek, she arrives at the much-talked-about 5th Avenue. She stops a couple walking passed her. "Hi. Can you tell me what street Port Authority is on?" she shouts out.

They shout back, "42nd Street," without stopping. But Jacq runs to them, as best she can with feet that are becoming harder to maneuver in a fast pace.

"Sorry. Just one more question," she calls out. The couple stops and turns around. "Can I get there by subway from here?"

The guy bobs his head about thinking it through. "Yeah," he says. "You can catch the blue line if you just keep walking down 5th. We'd walk you there, but we're only going another block-ish down." The real tragedy in that answer is that there's a stop for the N and R trains the other direction at 59th and 5th, but because this guy rarely uses that line, he doesn't think of it.

"Do you mind if I follow you that far?" she asks. He shrugs his shoulders saying "Sure" in body language. He and his girlfriend lead Jacq the next block and a half, until they reach Tiffany's.

"This is as far as we're going," he says.

Jacq looks up to see she's standing in front of one of the world's most iconic jewelry stores. "Tiffany's?" she says quizzically almost to herself. She looks back at the couple. "Are you buying 'special' jewelry?" she asks. The girl looks at her boyfriend with a gleam in her eye.

"I can neither confirm nor deny that today is the day that I shall ask the love of my life to be my bride," he says with a giant smile on his face.

"How wonderful," Jacq says momentarily forgetting about the cold and pain she's experiencing. "I wish you both the best of luck."

"Thanks. That's why we're doing it today. To add that extra bit of Christmas blessing on it," she pipes up to say.

Jacq slides back into her own reality with that. They are a lovely couple having a special Christmas together – a special New York Christmas at that. All she wants from the holiday or this city was her way home. She nods at the girlfriend. "Well good luck to the both of you again. I should be getting on my way," she says as she walks away. The couple hugs and enters the turning doors in the same slot together.

Trudging down 5th Avenue is in no way the pleasant experience that had been suggested by that man. Jacq has a greater appreciation and understanding of all the recommendations she got to pack some walking shoes and a coat. At this point she's walked another three blocks with no sight of a subway entrance. She's walking against a cold wind that makes what she faced on 58th Street seem like a light summer breeze. The buildings of 5th Avenue have created a wind tunnel that has strengthened the power and force of the cold air.

Jacq spots a group of tourists that are walking the same direction as she is. Then, she sees that they are reviewing a NYC Subway map. Without saying anything, she casually steps in closely behind them. Before she manages to get a glimpse of the map, the man puts it away. The group starts walking when the light changes on 54th Street. Immediately, Jacq notices a temperature difference. That group was blocking the horrible wind. She rushes to regain her position behind them. The next block is an easier walk. Her feet are still in pain, but she's gotten a break from the wind. At the intersection of 53rd and 5th, she nuzzles in between the group of tourists and another group waiting for the light to change. When everyone starts walking, she moves in the middle of all these people that seem to be moving like an amoeba down the avenue. Unfortunately, Jacq's respite from the wind also blocks her from seeing the subway entrance across the street. The group, who she thinks is going to the subway, continues their walk until they reach St. Patrick's Cathedral on 50th Street. When they start to walk up the stairs toward the Cathedral's doors, Jacq stops them.

"Where are you going?" she asks.

The group turns back with a look that screams, "Who are you?"

"You were holding a subway map. This isn't the subway," Jacq exclaims.

The group looks at each other and then to the man that was holding the map several blocks back when Jacq started to follow them. He looks back at the group and then to Jacq before saying, "Sorry miss, but it's the only map of the city we have. We didn't mean to mislead you. Would you like to join us for a privately led tour of the Cathedral? We have some extra passes."

Jacq drops her head in disappointment. She looks back up. "No," she mumbles. She turns and walks away continuing in the same direction downtown. The cold wind is back blowing colder and harder than before. She stops suddenly as she sees something that gives her hope. A smile relaxes her face. She walks even faster toward that hope. It's a sign that reads: Saks Fifth Avenue.

She practically runs into the store. Regardless of how she felt in the past about not needing winter clothes, now she not only needs them but greatly wants them. A doorman dressed in a red overcoat with green earmuffs says, "Merry Christmas. Can I help direct you toward the right department to finish your holiday shopping?"

"Coats and shoes," she blurts out.

Moments later, she is staring at racks of coats. She scans through the inventory, but nothing calls out to her. She is shivering, but nothing she sees makes her feel warm. She has been chilled to the bone and is staring at these coats like a grocery shopper that's just come off a week long fast. She circles at least ten racks as she makes her way to the back wall. That's where she comes to a complete stop. She's found it. The coat she never thought she'd want has become the apple of her eye. It's almost a replica of the sleeping bag coat the old woman back on Park Avenue was wearing, except this one is white. She takes it off the hanger and slides into it. It feels good. No, it feels great. She pulls the hood up over her head and snuggles into it.

"I see you've found something you like," a saleslady says from behind her. "Can I help you find anything else? A scarf ..."

"Shoes. Where are your shoes?" Jacq asks with no hesitation.

The saleslady looks down to see that Jacq has kicked her heels off. "I couldn't do it any more. Felt like knives stabbing my soles ... and soul for that matter," Jacq explains.

Smiling, the saleslady says, "Follow me."

In no time at all, Jacq is sitting in the Shoe Department wearing a pair of red UGG boots. She pulls a credit card out of her bag. As she hands it over she says, "Do you mind if I sit here while you ring it up? I'll be wearing both purchases out of the store."

"Absolutely," responds the saleslady. "If you'll give me your pumps, I'll put them in your UGG's box."

"I don't need the box or the pumps, but thank you," Jacq replies. "Oh, and gloves. I need gloves."

With the purchases made, Jacq steps back out into the cold New York City wind. In the time she's been inside, it has started to snow ever so lightly. Jacq bundles up even more so in her sleeping bag coat. She follows a group across the street into Rockefeller Center Plaza, where the famous Christmas tree stands above the ice skating rink every year. With warm, cushioned feet and a coat covering her head to toe, she has a new determination to get back to the airport and on a return flight to Phoenix as soon as possible. She darts in and out of the crowd of tourists, who are all enjoying the holiday festivities.

Jacq comes to the end of the plaza, where she has to make a right or left to keep going. She sees that to her left is the 48th Street sign, and to her right is 49th Street. Clearly she needs to make a left turn to continue her journey down to 42nd, but something more appealing catches her eye to the right – a coffee cart.

Two men are standing at the cart carrying on a conversation when Jacq approaches. The vendor running the cart looks up at her as she arrives. "Hey hon, what can I get you?" he asks.

"One coffee please," she answers.

"One cup of joe coming up," he says as he grabs a cup. "You want any cream or sugar?"

"Cream," she replies.

As the vendor goes through the motions of preparing her coffee, he turns around to his friend. "So they've been acting up all day?" he asks.

The man nods. "Yeah, I don't know what's wrong with them. But they've been spooked by something."

"It's Christmas Eve. Maybe they want to go fly with Santa," the vendor says with a chuckle.

"They're camels and donkeys, not reindeer you goof," the man says.

The vendor hands Jacq her coffee and says, "That'll be $2." As she reaches in her bag for the money he adds, "Have you been to see the Christmas show at Radio City? My friend here is one of the animal wranglers."

She acknowledges the wrangler with a nod and then gives the vendor the money. "No. It's not really my thing. Thanks for the coffee though." She looks back to the wrangler. "Hope your animals behave for you the rest of the day." And with that she turns and walks away down 49th Street. The men both shrug their shoulders and go back to their conversation.

Jacq is finally making headway. She walks past Radio City Music Hall, and even through Times Square barely noticing any of the spectacular decorations or that the snow has started falling harder and more steadily. All that she sees are street signs with numbers that are getting closer to 42nd Street and 8th Avenue.

Finally, she's there. Standing at the desired intersection, Jacq is beyond thrilled to see the big, brown brick building known as Port Authority. She hurries across the street. Just as she is about to enter, a tour guide stops her.

"Offering a special Christmas tour of the city. Last chance," he attempts to entice her.

"Not interested. Where can I get a bus to Newark Airport?" she asks. But before he can respond, she sees a sign directing her to the airport shuttles. With that, she rushes into the building.

"Merry Christmas … Mrs. Scrooge," he says as she disappears beyond the glass doors.

Chapter 6

The sky in Newark, NJ lacks cheer with its hue of dark gray. However, it gains an added flair from the bright white falling snow. The Phoenix gang, minus Jacq, is well settled into their seats. Alonya sits on the floor playing with her dolls and stuffed animals. She is between her dad and Nellie, who are sitting in the not-so-comfortable airport chairs. Across from Nellie is Holly, and to Holly's left is Charley, who is pretending to be asleep but in reality is far from resting.

Nellie keeps herself at peace and somewhat rested by humming to herself and watching people walk by. Alonya looks up to her new friend. "Are you singing again?" she asks.

"I'm humming, but it's along the same lines," Nellie replies.

"Why do you sing so much?" Alonya asks.

"Alonya!" Frank exclaims as he breaks away from reading a book.

"Leave her alone," Nellie tells Frank. "She's young and curious. Questions are a good thing." She turns her attention back to Alonya, who is looking up at her with a delightful smile that can only come from a child. "I suppose I sing because that's what singers do," Nellie answers.

Holly looks up from the Paula Deen magazine that Charley bought her at the Hudson News in the airport. "Are you an actual singer?" she asks Nellie.

"I used to sing professionally if that's what you mean by actual," Nellie replies, not really liking the question.

"Really? That is so neat," Holly exclaims.

Charley ends his mock nap. He leans into the conversation. "Do you sing in Phoenix somewhere I may have heard you? Your voice sounds familiar to me, but I just can't nail where I've heard you," he says.

"I don't know where you may have heard me, but I sang here," Nellie answers.

"In the airport?" Alonya asks with a mixture of shock and excitement.

Nellie laughs. "In New York City."

"Were you on Broadway with your name up in lights and all?" Holly asks.

"No to Broadway, but my name was in lights a few times. I was a blues and jazz singer. Played every main stage and club in Manhattan," Nellie explains.

This sparks another familiar chord for Charley, but he still doesn't have the answer. Knowing he knows the answer only adds to the frustration. The frustration is a nice break from his worrying about how to tell Holly that he lost his job, however.

"What took you to Phoenix?" Frank asks Nellie.

"My husband's health. The doctors said the desert air would be better for him. We lived many happy years in Arizona," Nellie says almost to herself.

"Where's your husband now? Didn't he want to go with you to Detroit?" Alonya asks.

"He's with your mother among the angels," Nellie replies.

"I'm in Arizona because of my husband too, but there's no way I'd stay if he wasn't there," Holly chimes in.

Charley bows his head avoiding eye contact with anyone. Nellie looks at him and then back to Holly responding, "That's because you're still married to the idea of being in Arkansas. Things were different for me. When Albert passed away fifteen years ago, Phoenix was home to me. My days of playing the stages of the Big Apple were behind me. And my days of being a nurse were really behind me," she says while looking down at Holly's stomach. Holly follows Nellie's eye line. She nervously looks away.

"You were a nurse, too?" Frank asks. "Sounds like you've done a little bit of everything."

"I don't know about everything, but I did what I needed to do to support myself, and then I had a nice chunk of time when I was blessed to earn a living doing something I loved. I'm very pleased with the life I've had and continue to have," Nellie says.

"How many years were you and Albert married?" Charley asks.

"We came together later in life than you and Holly did. I was probably ten years older than you are now when we got married, but we still had twenty-three wonderful years together," she responds.

"What advice do you have for a young couple like us only one year in?" Charley asks.

"Communication is a key element," Nellie replies. "People often get caught up in the mistaken belief that they can save a loved one's feelings with what they call a white lie, but a lie is a lie no matter what other words you put in front of it. Our contract with God, that's what I call the Bible, says that the truth shall set you free."

Getting the message, Holly nervously changes the subject. "With all this sitting and waiting, I about forgot that today's a holiday. Will you sing us a Christmas song, Nellie?"

Nellie looks around at all the people in the airport. Outside of their group of five, everyone else seems engulfed in their own ways of waiting. Some are reading, while others are tuned into music, TV, and movies on their various forms of electronic devices. Some have fallen to sleep, while others are very busy keeping little ones occupied with games and a lot of walking around answering the question, "What's that?"

over and over. She looks back over to Holly and says, "Maybe later."

The now familiar sound of the airport's intercom system echoes through the corridor. An announcer says, "Ladies and gentlemen. At this time we are beginning the boarding process for Flight 1340 to Northwest Arkansas at Gate 25A."

Holly bolts upright in her seat. She looks to Charley with much excitement. "You hear that?" she asks.

Charley shrugs his shoulders. "Yeah, but …"

"If we get to Bentonville, Aunt Edith will drive us to Momma's," she insists.

Charley perks up a little hearing this suggestion. "It's worth a shot. Sure is a whole lot closer than we are now," he says while standing up.

Frank, who has missed this whole exchange due to his reading, looks up. "I thought you guys were flying to D.C. first," he says.

"Ah, but fate is with us my friend. Where we really need to get to is Arkansas. And that plane right there is heading our direction. We've been saved," Charley exclaims as he collects their things and helps Holly out of her seat.

"Good luck. Merry Christmas to the both of you," Frank says before going back to his reading.

"Merry Christmas to all of you," Nellie says as she gently puts her hand on Holly's stomach.

"I think you're our good luck charm, Nellie. It was a real pleasure meeting you," Charley says.

"It was a pleasure meeting you too," Nellie responds. "Maybe we can get together back in Phoenix after the holidays."

Charley nervously looks over to the gate to see people lined up for boarding. He looks back to Nellie. "Ah, yeah. That sounds like a great idea," he says with no conviction. He puts his arm around Holly. "You ready?"

"Oh my gosh, yes. This is just perfect," she answers.

Alonya hops up to give Holly a hug. "Thanks for playing with me. Your baby is going to have a really fun mom," she adds.

Holly hugs her back, touched by the little girl's sweetness. "I know I've already said it, but I hope my baby is just like you," she tells Alonya. Then she shifts back under her husband's arm and they walk away.

At the gate for the Northwest Arkansas flight, Charley and Holly impishly join the line of the boarding passengers. The line is moving seemingly faster than normal. Holly looks up to see Charley grinning ear to ear. He kisses her on the forehead. There are only a few people between them and the entrance onto the plane, then two, then one … then Charley lifts his hand to show the boarding agent their passes. He attempts to keep walking, but ….

"Wait sir. I have to scan your passes, " the agent says.

Charley bows his head, beaten. He turns around and hands them to her. The agent puts the first pass's barcode under the scanner. "Ble THUNK," the machine sounds off. After a second try, the agent inspects the passes.

"These boarding passes are for the flight to Washington D.C. This isn't your flight," she explains as she hands the passes back to Charley.

He hands them back to her showing the second set of passes. "But if you go to the ticket right behind that one, you'll see that we're ultimately going to Arkansas. So, this is exactly the right flight for us," he suggests with a little extra charm poured into his words.

She looks and then attempts to hand them back to him, but he steps back. With a forced smile she says, "Yes sir. That's a ticket for a plane that leaves out of D.C. This is not that plane."

Holly steps around Charley. With a sense of desperation in her voice she says, "Please let us go. You can see that's where we're supposed to end up."

"Even if this flight weren't full, your Arkansas ticket is going to a different airport. You're going to have to wait for your D.C. flight," the agent explains as she places the boarding passes in Holly's hands.

"Do you know when our plane is going to start boarding?" Charley asks.

"I'm sure it will be soon," the agent responds as she reaches for the boarding passes of the people standing behind the deflated couple.

They walk away saddened. As they reach the corridor, Charley's cell phone rings. He reaches in his pocket and silences the phone.

"How do you know you didn't want to talk to whoever that was?" Holly asks.

"I don't know. It's was probably a telemarketer, and I'm just not in the mood right now," he says avoiding eye contact with her.

Holly spots a ladies room ahead. "Here, will you hold my stuff. I should go before we go sit back down at the other gate," she asks while walking away not waiting for him to answer.

Charley takes out his cell. The screen reads: *Missed Call – Work.* He clears the screen and puts the phone back in his pocket.

Back at the D.C. gate, Alonya looks up from playing with her dolls and sees Jacq wind in and out of people in the crowded corridor. "It's Jacq the lady!" she exclaims.

Frank's face brightens. He stands up to greet her. "Hi," he says. Jacq stops, startled.

"Hi. You're having a long layover," she assumes.

"Yeah. Unfortunately, we've been delayed because of the snow," he explains.

"Really? I would think Newark could handle a little snow," she says.

"Yeah, but our plane's been stuck somewhere else all day," he replies. He steps back to inspect her new winter outfit. "I see you went shopping."

"What can I say? The choice was between stylish or warm. I chose warm," she says while posing to show off her big coat.

Alonya pops around from behind her dad. "How was your meeting? Did my hug bring you luck?" she asks hopefully.

"I wish I could say yes," Jacq answers.

"Sorry to hear that. Hope it wasn't because of the tweaks I added," Frank offers.

Jacq reaches out and touches his arm. "Not at all. I never even got to take my laptop out of the bag," she says. "I'd love to talk, but I'm hoping to make up for the bad day by catching an earlier flight back to Phoenix." She turns to leave.

"Wait," Frank calls out.

She turns back around. Frank reaches into his pocket and pulls out a business card. He hands it to her. "I was beating myself up for not giving this to you before."

She reads the card, and then looks back up at him. "I'll look you up for some graphic designs in the future," she says with a smile.

"I hope you'll look me up for dinner," he replies.

Her smile broadens before she turns and rushes away.

In the ladies room, Holly exits a stall. She is surprised to see Nellie standing at a sink washing her hands. Nellie looks up into the mirror, "What are you doing here?" she asks.

"They wouldn't let us on the plane," Holly explains.

While taking some makeup out of her purse, Nellie asks, "So, how long have you been in labor?"

Holly's head darts in Nellie's direction, "What?"

"My many years of living have completely erased my ability to beat around the bush. How far apart are your contractions?" Nellie asks again, this time meeting Holly eye to eye.

Trying to shake it off, Holly goes back touching up her makeup. "Contractions? No. I'm only seven months pregnant," she says.

"Like I said earlier, before I sang professionally, I was a nurse. I've helped deliver a lot of babies, and I know yours is on the way out," Nellie replies.

Holly shakes her head. "I'm fine. I've just got to get to Arkansas. My baby is going to be born at home. My true Christmas miracle," she adds. "I'll see you back at the gate." Holly quickly stuffs her makeup back in her bag and leaves the bathroom.

* * * * * *

At the Phoenix gate, Jacq approaches a clerk typing away on a computer. She slides up to the counter with a little flirt in her voice. "Hi. I'm hoping you can help me turn what's been a bad day into a good one."

Taken by her beauty, the man says, "Usually I'd say I doubt it, but in your case I hope so."

She hands him her boarding pass. "I'm booked on a flight later tonight, but I would kill to get on this one instead."

"Things are pretty tight today, but let me see if there are any options for you," he says. He starts typing on the computer, but is interrupted by the phone ringing. He reaches for the phone while mouthing, "Excuse me" to Jacq. "Hello?" he says. "Hm-mm," he responds and he goes back to searching for a way to help Jacq. He stops suddenly. "You've got to be kidding," he exasperates into the phone. "Okay," he finishes before hanging up.

The clerk looks at his co-worker. "Buckle up. Ugly just arrived," he says. Then he looks back to Jacq. "Do you have a membership to the airline's VIP club?" he asks.

"No. Why? Will that get me out of here faster?" she asks.

Then the airport's sound system squeaks before the announcer says, "Ladies and gentlemen, may I have your attention. Due to severe winter weather all flights have been cancelled. The airport is officially closed for the night. I repeat, the tarmac is closed for the night. All flights have been cancelled. Merry Christmas."

Chapter 7

The Phoenix group, minus Jacq, has all settled back into their seats at the D.C. gate. Charley consoles a sobbing Holly. "First, we were going to spend Christmas in hot Arizona. Now we have to sleep on the cold floor in an airport," she cries. "We're going to miss it all together."

"It's okay. We're going to make this work. We'll get out first thing in the morning and still be at your mom's on Christmas day," he offers.

Alonya looks up at her father. "Are we going to miss Christmas too?" she asks.

"No," he assures her. "It won't be the same as usual, but we won't miss it." He can see that his little girl isn't convinced. "You know what? I think we could use a round of hot dogs and fries for everyone. What do you think?"

Alonya perks up. "Yeah," she exclaims.

Frank looks at Nellie. "I'm guessing hot dogs aren't your style, but do you think there's anything else you might want? I'm happy to stop at another place for you," he offers.

"I'd prefer a turkey dog if it's a choice, but either way I'll take one with everything on it," she replies.

Amused and somewhat shocked by her response, Frank laughs and then asks, "Anything to drink?"

"I'd love a lemonade if they have it," she answers.

Frank turns to Charley and Holly. "Would you guys like to join us for hot dogs? My treat," he offers.

Charley looks to Holly for her answer. She contemplates, rubs her stomach, and then says, "That sounds good. I just want ketchup on mine ... and a large order of fries ... and a Coke ... no, water. I'll take a water."

"And how about you?" Frank asks Charley.

Charley stands. "Why don't I go and help you carry it all back," he suggests.

Frank nods accepting the offer. He turns to Alonya, who is back on the floor playing with her stuffed animals. "Can you pack those up until we get back?" he asks his daughter.

"I want to stay here and play. Miss Nellie, Holly, and the baby will be here with me," she says.

Nellie can see he is unsure. "She'll be fine here with me, if you're all right with it," Nellie offers.

"Please …." Alonya says going full throttle with charm.

"I think it will be okay, though it does remind me of one of those bad parenting choices you hear about on the news," he says.

Charley extends his hand. "Can I have your cell for a minute?" he asks. Frank reaches in his pocket and hands it over. Charley takes it and dials a number. Suddenly a ring comes from Charley's pants pocket. He reaches in, takes his phone out, and presses a button to silence it. Then he hands his phone to Holly. "There. If she needs you, she can call from my phone or vice versa," he says.

Frank smiles as he takes his phone back. That seems like a perfect modern day solution. He and Charley head off.

Over at the Phoenix gate, Jacq is on her cell phone. "Seriously? LaGuardia, Kennedy, Philadelphia are all closed? How is that possible?" she asks exasperated. "I'll rent a car and drive to wherever. Just find me a way to get home." There's a long pause before she hangs up the phone and leans her forehead against a nearby column. She stays that way for a few minutes, though it feels much longer. And then she starts speaking out loud. First it's soft, but she gets louder as she repeats it over and over until she lifts her head to stand up straight again.

"No, no, no, no – this is not my day. This is ridiculous," she declares as she reaches to put her cell phone in her coat pocket, but she stops. Her face looks quizzical as she tries to detect what she's touching. She pulls it out. It's Frank's business card. She stares at it for a moment. Her contemplative look shifts to a smile. Then she takes her cell phone back out and dials the number listed on the card.

At the hot dog stand, Frank's phone rings. He takes it out of his pocket. He sees that it's a number from Phoenix he doesn't recognize. Assuming that Alonya changed her mind after he got out of her sight, he answers saying, "Hey baby. Did you change your mind after you couldn't see me anymore?" he asks.

Jacq is speechless. She is hit with two thoughts at the same time – how did he know my number? And, that's an awfully presumptuous tone to take with a woman you haven't been on a date with yet. She thinks about hanging up, but instinctively says, "Umm, not exactly."

He pulls the phone away from his ear to look at the number. He still doesn't recognize it, but now knows it isn't Charley's phone. He is mortified as he asks, "Ahhh, I'm sorry. Who is this?"

Jacq is relieved that he wasn't coming on to her with a sleazy attitude. "Hi, this is Jacq the lady, as your daughter refers to me," she answers.

Frank doubles over in embarrassment. Charley looks back. "Are you okay, buddy?" he asks.

He nods affirmatively as he stands back up. He holds up a finger to indicate he needs a minute as he steps out of line. Redirecting his attention to the phone, he says, "Wow, that was the worst possible way to answer your call. I'm really, really sorry. I thought it was Alonya. She's back at …"

Jacq cuts him off. "It's okay. I'm glad it was your daughter instead of another dinner date you were thinking of," she says, almost shocking herself with her flirtation. "And, um, speaking of that, it looks like I'm stuck here in

Newark as well. So, I thought I'd call to take you up on that dinner offer."

Frank looks back at the hot dog stand, and then at Charley, who has found a chair and put his head down. "Yeah, that's great. The only thing is …." he stops himself. "It's not the classy dinner I hoped to give you, but how do you feel about a hot dog and dinner with the group you flew here with? I've kind of already offered to buy dinner for everyone. In fact, I was in line to buy the food when you called. I know it's not ideal, but …"

"Sounds great. I like relish, onions, and mustard on mine," she says.

Frank relaxes. With a great big smile he says, "Sounds good. I may get the same. Why don't you meet me back over where we saw you when I gave you my card. I'll have your dinner when I see you next."

She hangs up satisfied. This isn't in any way the day she planned or would've planned, but now that she's in it, it feels like it just might have the promise of something good.

Frank gets back in line. Charley joins him. "Everything okay?" Charley asks.

"Yeah. Disaster adverted. We'll have one more joining us," he answers.

They slowly make their way to the front of the line. With the large order made and then collected, the two guys head back.

As Jacq slowly walks toward the girls, Alonya again looks up and sees her coming. Just like before, she jumps up and says, "It's Jacq the lady again."

Alonya takes off running toward her. Nellie starts to react, but recognizes Jacq. Alonya hugs Jacq again. Jacq is still taken aback by the affection, but less so than the first time.

"Have you come to join us?" Nellie asks.

"Yes. I didn't manage to get out either. I spoke to Frank. So now I at least get to join you guys for hot dogs," Jacq says.

Nellie moves the bags out of the seat next to her. She stands up. "There happens to be a seat for you right here," she offers.

"Oh no. You don't have to get up," Jacq says.

"I don't have to, but I'm doing it all the same. I think this seat is better for you. So, I'm going to slide over one," she responds with a wink.

Jacq accepts the seat, and the support Nellie is offering. She takes off her big coat, folds it, and places it under the seat with her briefcase satchel. She looks over to Nellie, who is still wearing her full-length chinchilla that she's had on all day. "Aren't you too warm wearing that inside?" Jacq asks.

"I don't get too warm. That's why I'm so at home in Arizona. Now cold, that I can get, and that I don't want to get. So I always appreciate being warm. I said I'd never go back to Detroit in the winter, but here I am on that journey.

Goes to show we should never say never. You just invite yourself to be proven wrong," Nellie explains.

Across the aisle, Holly is resting with her eyes closed when Charley's phone chimes. She looks at it and sees that the screen has a message saying a new text message has come in. She presses a button, and the screen goes blank. "Oh no. Don't do that," she begs the phone. She looks toward Jacq. "Do you know how to do this?" she asks.

"Do what?" Jacq asks.

"My husband's phone said it had a text message. I tried to open it, but it disappeared instead," she answers as she hands the phone over to Jacq.

"Hot dogs!" rings out from behind them as Frank and Charley approach. Alonya jumps up ready to indulge. The ladies smile because everyone is ready for a little comfort food at this point in their day.

"Good. You know your phone better than I do," Jacq says as she hands Charley his phone.

"What's wrong with the phone?" he asks.

"A text message came in, but it disappeared when I tried to open it," Holly explains.

"Oh," he says with a bit of concern. "I'll take care of it … just as soon as we sort out who gets what out of these bags," he says very happy to have something to divert the attention to.

Charley and Frank hand out hot dogs, fries, and drinks to everyone with a nice helping of paper napkins to go around.

Before sitting down, Charley pulls up the text message without anyone noticing. It's from Neal, a friend from work. It reads: *Dude, you have really messed up. For your sake, I hope someone's dead or really sick.* He quickly tucks the phone away in his pocket and settles in next to Holly.

Comfort food tastes good all the time, thus the whole comfort element of the title. But in stressful times, it tastes even better. It eases the mind, relaxes the body, and gives a respite to the soul. Though there is still a frenzied swarm of other stranded passengers around them, for a moment, this group is at peace as they enjoy some good old-fashioned junk food.

"This is so good. Thanks again Frank," Holly says breaking the silence. "I still can't believe we're going to miss Christmas."

"We're not missing it. It's just going to be different," Charley says.

"That's what I mean. We're not going to get to do any of the things that makes Christmas, Christmas," she responds.

"Connotations," Nellie says.

Everyone turns to her. "What's that Miss Nellie?" Charley asks.

"She's caught up in the connotations of Christmas. Everyone has their own connection to the holiday. What it means to them. The only way any of us can miss it is if we're not breathing on December 25. Otherwise Christmas is going to happen on schedule just like it does every year. Our flights may be off schedule. Our activities may be off schedule. But Christmas will come whether we're where we think we should be or not," Nellie explains.

"But will Santa come to the airport?" Alonya asks Nellie.

"Well baby, Santa may have to drop your stuff off somewhere else. Or he may drop off something here and leave some at your grandparents. Either way, you'll get everything that Santa intends for you to have. But, Christmas is about more than just the toys and gifts," Nellie says.

"You mean baby Jesus?" Alonya asks.

"That's definitely a big part of it in my book, but what I'm saying is that everyone has memories of what they've done before. And if someone does the same thing for a lot of years in a row, they tend to start thinking that's what Christmas is. I usually go to church at Christmas. So that's part of what Christmas means to me. But I have Jewish friends who have their own connotation of Christmas. For them, it means a day of Chinese food and going to see a movie. And Holly here, she's attached to Christmas as something that happens in Arkansas."

Frank puts his arm around his daughter. "She's right honey. I used to have so much fun when I was your age at Christmas. And I've kept going home every year, but after you were born it took on a whole new meaning for me. When you were a baby and couldn't even talk yet, your face lit up the first time you saw a decorated tree. After that, I couldn't wait until this time of the year came around just so I could see that look on your face again as you stared at the sparkling lights."

"We all have special memories. And the great thing about memories is that we can share them. And in doing so, we get to relive them. We get to picture those special moments, hear those joyful sounds, and even smell the pine or cookies or whatever happens to be a part of our individual stories," Nellie says. Then she looks at Holly. "Why don't you tell us about those special moments you think you're missing? Make them part of this day by sharing them with us."

Holly shrinks back in her seat, suddenly at a loss for words. "I don't know," she says. "It's just better there, I guess. You know, with my family. I've always woken up in my momma's house on Christmas morning."

"You woke up there a lot of mornings, but there's something special about waking up there on Christmas morning for you. What do you think it is? What do you think of when you picture yourself opening your eyes on Christmas morning?" Nellie asks.

"I never thought of it like that," Holly says. She smiles, and the tension in her shoulders seems to soften. "There's a smell of country ham, and fresh baked bread. My mom and her sisters are whispering. One telling the other to grab a casserole dish or stir the grits. It's still dark outside, but it's the one morning I'm excited to get up early. It's finally time to open the presents that have teased me for weeks. Of course, there's still more waiting because we have to have the family breakfast first," she remembers.

Charley puts his arm around Holly. "That is one good breakfast too. Scrambled eggs plus egg casserole, sausage, bacon, and big cuts of beautiful brown salty country ham sit in the center of the table. There's homemade biscuits, and jam that someone made and jarred back in the summer. Heck, it's the one day a year that even the dog gets a fresh cooked meal," he says while lost in his thoughts.

"You're making me hungry, and I'm still eating my hot dog," Jacq says with a laugh.

Holly leans even closer to Charley. "He didn't know what to do with himself the first time he joined us. And I couldn't believe that he hadn't grown up doing the same thing," she says.

"Shoot, the closest thing to a meal we got on Christmas day was a sandwich or some warmed up leftovers. We did all our celebrating the night before. My brother and I would get up and play with our toys, but my parents stayed in bed 'til at least lunchtime," he explains. "The whole idea of a family gathering at six o'clock in the morning was not even considered at my house."

"Me too," Nellie says with a hearty laugh. "For years, my saying was I don't do breakfast cause I'm not up 'til lunch. In my New York years, we'd all gather at the jazz club late on Christmas Eve and sing and party our way to dawn. Those were great years," she says wistfully. She turns her attention back to Holly. "That's what I mean. I can still enjoy those memories without needing to keep on doing the exact same thing. Once Albert and I moved to Phoenix, our Christmas plans changed. Our church has a special midnight service that we started going to. It's a simple service that only lasts thirty minutes or so. The minister tells the Christmas story, we pray, take communion, and sing The First Noel at midnight. Then most of the families head home. But that first year Albert and I were missing our jazz club friends. He asked a few of our new friends from church if they'd like to go to an all night diner. Several joined us, and that became our new tradition. Even now that Albert's gone on, after the midnight service some friends and I head over to the diner and spend most of the night sharing each other's company with our stories."

"Are you sad you won't be at the diner tonight?" Holly asked.

"Not even a little bit," Nellie responds. "I've been blessed with the acquaintance of all of you. No idea what will happen between now and morning, but I know that God is with me blessing me all along the way." She turns toward Jacq. "How about you, sweet thing?"

Jacq looks around to see if Nellie is possibly talking to someone else. But all eyes are on her. "Ahh, what about me?" she asks.

"What's your Christmas story?" Holly asks.

"Oh, I, I don't have one," she says. "No offense. It sounds like you guys all really love this holiday. That's cool, holidays just aren't my thing."

"I've never met anybody that didn't celebrate Christmas," Charley pipes in.

"Are you Jewish?" Holly asks.

"No. I'm religion and holiday neutral," Jacq responds.

"So not just Christmas, you don't celebrate any holiday?" Charley asks astonished.

Frank can see this is making Jacq uncomfortable. He would like to hear the answers as much as everyone, but then he sees Alonya has fallen asleep in his lap. He uses this to rescue Jacq. "Sorry for changing the subject, but while my girl is asleep, do you guys have any advice on how I'm going to pull off Christmas morning and Santa's visit at the airport?"

"Santa will take care of Santa, as will Christmas morning take care of itself," says Nellie.

"But I mean gift ideas. I had everything shipped to my parents' house. I've got to have some kind of a surprise for Alonya when she wakes up in the morning," Frank explains further.

"Why don't you and Jacq go check out some of the shops while Alonya is napping. I'll stay here with her," Nellie offers.

There are numerous reasons why this sounds like a good idea to Frank, but it all boils down to boy likes girl and hopes said girl likes boy. He looks to Jacq. "I know you got more than your share of walking earlier, but want to join me? I could use a woman's perspective on finding the perfect little girl gift in an airport," he suggests.

A knowing smile creases Jacq's face. "Sure," she says.

Jacq takes her purse out of her brief case. She looks toward Nellie. "It's okay to leave my coat and briefcase here?"

"Of course," she replies.

Before Frank and Jacq walk away, a white man in his mid-fifties approaches the group. "I'm really sorry to interrupt, but I had to come over to meet you. I've been a fan for years," he says.

Frank, Jacq, Holly, and Charley all look at one another curiously, and then back to the man. Nellie extends her hand to the gentleman. "It's very nice to meet you," she says.

The four continue to watch this exchange. They know Nellie said she used to be a singer in New York clubs, but they never thought of it in terms of her having fans. How could this man recognize her so many years later? The man hands his boarding pass over to Nellie. "Would you sign the back of this? Sorry I don't have something better than that," he offers.

"Believe me when I tell you I've signed a lot worse, and turned down signing a few other things through the years," she says with a laugh.

She signs the paper and hands it back to him. "Thank you Miss Clark. It was a genuine pleasure to run across you here. This is a very special Christmas gift to me. Are you staying the night here like the rest of us commoners?" he asks.

"It looks that way," she answers.

"Well, I'll be roaming around. Can't really sleep in airports. So if you need anything, it would be my honor to go get it for you," he offers.

"Thank you, but I'm well taken care of," she explains while gesturing to the two couples that are utterly baffled by this point.

"Again, it was such a pleasure to meet you," the man says before walking away.

Nellie looks up to the frozen stares of all four of her new friends. "Aren't you going shopping?" she asks Frank.

"That man just asked for your autograph," Frank says.

"And he called you Miss Clark," Jacq adds.

"Yes. He did both of those things," Nellie replies.

Charley's face shifts from a look of total confusion to complete amazement. "Holy mother of all that's good, you are Stella Clark," he exclaims. "I knew there was something familiar about your voice. How did I miss that? I mean I've been hanging out with you all day. Sat next to you on the plane, then here, wow ...."

Frank and Jacq start to get excited by Charley's realization. They look at each other, then to Charley, and then to Nellie. Jacq asks, "Why were you flying coach?"

"Because that's the plane ticket that was available," she responds.

Holly, who has been sort of lying down in her seat against Charley, struggles to sit upright. She turns to look at her husband. "You've met Nellie before?"

He shakes his head. "No, Nellie here is actually the great Stella Clark," he explains.

Holly still hasn't caught up to everyone else's realization. She looks to Nellie. "Your name isn't Nellie?" she asks.

"My name absolutely is Nellie. It's just that some people know me by that other name," she explains.

Charley can see that Holly is still not clued in. He says, "Honey, remember that Christmas album I played for you? The one that had all the bluesy songs on it?"

"Yeah, but ...," she stops as she finally catches up to the rest of the group. She jerks her head toward Nellie. "You're famous!" she exclaims.

Nellie holds her hand up to calm Holly. "I used to be, but there's no reason to draw attention to the past when the present has us stuck in this wide open space with nowhere to go."

Holly lowers her voice to a whisper and speaks slower as though that too will lower the volume. "Oh my gosh! You... are... faaaammmooouuusssss! What are you doing here?"

"The same thing you are my dear, traveling to see family for the holidays."

Frank turns to Charley saying, "I would've guessed you more of a country music fan."

"'Cause of this twang in my accent?" Charley asks with a wink. "My dad is a huge blues fan. Says it's got the stories of country music, but sung from the soul of real storytellers." Charley looks toward Nellie in earnest. "Your Christmas album is by far my all time favorite."

She chuckles as she says, "You are one of a very small group." Alonya stirs, but rolls over in her dad's lap. Nellie points at Alonya as she says to Frank, "You might want to get that shopping trip started."

Frank nods in agreement. He slowly takes off his jacket and folds it so that the lining faces out to make a softer pillow for Alonya. He gently gets up while placing his jacket under her head. After waiting a moment to make sure that she isn't going to wake up, he gives a nod to Jacq. She gets up to join him. Before Frank can even ask, Nellie moves over into the seat next to Alonya. "She'll be fine. Go," she directs Frank.

Frank and Jacq head off in hopes of making his little girl's Christmas special from the offerings of the airport's shopping mall.

Chapter 8

With thousands of passengers stuck in Newark for the night, the terminal is stacked with people. Parents try to keep toddlers busy allowing them to run back and forth in the corridors. The restaurants all have lines that will likely take hours to clear up, if at all. The stores are full of shoppers looking for gifts that will make do until they can get to their luggage or final destinations.

Jacq stops in front of an electronics kiosk. She points out a small gadget that would put Alonya a touch away from the music, movie, or television show of her choosing. Frank points out the $200 price tag. "She's seven," he says.

They walk into a bookstore. While Jacq peruses the magazines and best selling novels, Frank makes his way back to the children's section. The store looks like it's at the end of a going out of business sale. There is only a small selection left on the almost empty shelves. Jacq walks up behind him. "Looks like this section has been cleaned out too," she says. Frank nods his head and stands. They walk back out into the corridor.

Curiosity wins out. Frank asks, "You said that Christmas isn't your thing. Did your family not celebrate it or is that something you started as an adult?"

"No, we celebrated Christmas ... we used to anyway," she says while looking away.

He sees that she's as uncomfortable now as she was when the group started asking her questions about this earlier. "I'm sorry. I shouldn't have asked. I appreciate you helping me look for a gift for Alonya, especially if you don't like the holiday," he says.

She shakes her head. "Christmas used to be my favorite time of year. My family had so many activities. We needed a vacation to rest from all the stuff we did, but that all ended," she explains. "My sister was killed in a car accident a few years ago on Thanksgiving night. Our holiday season normally would've kicked off the following day with Black Friday shopping. And I don't mean we would've gone to a store or two. Every year, we were at our first store by 6am and kept going until well after dark. We hit the main shopping spots in Phoenix and often popped up to Scottsdale too."

"That's some serious shopping," he responds. "I'm lucky to have such a pro helping me. Never been much of a shopper myself."

"We usually had it planned out days or even weeks ahead of time, but that all came to a crashing halt ..." Jacq stops. "Crashing ... that's a bad choice of words."

He places his arm around her shoulder. Jacq is surprised, but touched. She rests against him. "You don't have to talk about this if it's too sad or uncomfortable for you," he offers.

"It's actually nice. In Phoenix, I've managed to avoid most holiday functions using work as an excuse. Really, that's what I was doing with this business trip. But it seems that Christmas refuses to be ignored this year. It has been hammering at me all day. Everywhere I turned this afternoon in the city, there was someone else telling me how lucky I was to be there at Christmas. You even said it," she adds. "Then, I get back here just in time to be snowed in, and find respite with a group ... that decides to share Christmas stories. I've been in sales long enough to know when a no is opening up to a yes. And that's where I find myself here with you, and our whole group back there. What Nellie said about letting yourself enjoy the Christmas you have instead of insisting on having the past repeat itself, that resonated with me," Jacq says with a new, more relaxed smile.

"That's good," Frank responds. "I mean it's good that you're going to allow yourself to have it again. Doesn't sound like your sister would've wanted you to give up Christmas for her."

"It was because of her, but it wasn't for her. It was .... You know what, it doesn't matter. We're here, now. This is our time to find something for your daughter. Let's do that," she says while starting to walk again.

Not wanting to push her to talk about anything she doesn't want to, Frank joins her in walking toward the next store. But Jacq stops again. "When did your wife die?" she asks.

That's a question he wasn't expecting. He struggles to put his words together as he says, "Um, it was, ah ... ten months ago."

"Is that too soon for you to start dating again? I mean I know this isn't a date, but it feels like a date-ish kind of thing happening. Am I wrong?" she asks.

"It feels date-ish to me. Is that okay with you?" he returns the question.

She thinks about her answer before saying, "Yes. I think so. Can't say I've ever started a relationship out with anyone this way before. Of course then none of the other relationships worked out, so something totally different is good." Then she realizes she just said out loud that this was a possible relationship. She shakes her head in embarrassment. "Not that we're anywhere near being in a relationship. I mean ... I don't know what I mean. Maybe we should just get back to shopping." She starts walking again, but stops again before Frank has even gotten started. "The thing is, what I was wondering, kind of concerned about actually, are you ready to be dating someone if you're still mourning?"

"No," Frank spouts out. "I mean, yes I'm ready. I'm not mourning. I mean I guess I am, but not like you think." He stops. Then he tries another tactic. "What's the simplest way to explain this?" he thinks aloud.

Jacq stops him. "Don't. You don't owe me an answer to a question I shouldn't have asked." She turns to start walking again, but he reaches out and takes her hand to stop her.

"No wait," he says. "I don't mind explaining. It deserves an explanation." Jacq, tingling over that good feeling that comes from two palms fitting so nicely in each other's clasp, meets him eye to eye. "Rosa, that's my ex. Well, not ex, my deceased wife. But that sounds so morbid and dreary. Anyway, she was my best friend, but we were never in love. We met at work, and became fast friends. She liked the same restaurants I did, so we started having lunch together every day. We both liked old movies, so we would go to special screenings when we could find them. But we weren't dating. There was never that romantic spark," he says before taking a pause. "So why did we end up married, you must be asking yourself."

"Sort of," Jacq admits.

"Turns out Rosa's parents crossed the boarder illegally when she was a baby. They settled in Colorado. Rosa grew up there, graduated high school, graduated college, all without ever knowing about her citizenship status. It wasn't until her mom died that she found out about everything. By then she had moved to Phoenix. She and I had become friends and ...," he pauses trying to keep this explanation as simple as possible, but wanting to fully explain things. "Her dad had passed away a few years before, but her mom was there to take care of everything. But with her mom, it was Rosa's responsibility. That's when she learned that her parent's were illegal aliens, and that since she had been born in Mexico, she too was here illegally. With all the crackdowns on immigration, she was suddenly in danger of being sent back to a country she didn't even know she'd ever been to. Her family had cut off all ties with their old life to avoid being caught. Technically she had family there, but no one she knew. She spoke enough of the language to get by in the U.S., but not well enough to carry on full conversations. Long story short, I married her, she got to stay in the only

114

country she'd ever known as home, and we planned to divorce after we'd been married long enough to make everything legal."

"And Alonya? Was she part of the legalization plan?" Jacq asks.

"No, Alonya wasn't part of any plan. Alonya was about as unplanned as unplanned can be. I mean I'm grateful that it happened, because she's my reason to breathe now," he says. "But ... there was a drunken New Year's Eve right before we were about to be divorced. We celebrated the New Year and celebrated Rosa's new freedom of getting back to the life she was living before her mom passed away. We never even shared a bed the whole time we were married, but that night we did. And that night, we made Alonya."

"And then Rosa died?" Jacq asks.

"It was one of those things they say you can never prepare for. We had breakfast together. I left to drop Alonya off at day care, and Rosa should've been at work by the time I got there. But I got into the office and no Rosa. I called her cell phone, no answer. Called the house, nothing. I called the police to see if there'd been any wrecks matching her car's description, but there was nothing. So I went back home, and found her in the garage. As she was getting into the car, she suffered an aneurysm. The doctors said it killed her instantly."

Jacq nods. "Okay, I have delved far enough into your business for one day. Let's go find Miss Alonya a gift before all the rest of the shelves are emptied out." She turns to start walking, but he stops her again.

"Feel free to delve anytime you want. We may be stuck in the airport, but this has turned into the best day I've had in a long time," he says.

They smile at one another. He leans in to kiss her, but the moment is interrupted by Holly's voice. "Have ya'll found Alonya anything yet?" They turn to see Holly walking up behind them, pulling her suitcase along.

"Not yet," Frank says. "Is everything okay back there?"

"Yeah. Alonya woke up, but she's fine. She's re-introducing Charley and Nellie to all her stuffed animals. I had to go to the bathroom, again. And thought I should touch up my makeup," indicating why she's has her carry-on for a bathroom trip.

There's a brief awkward moment where Frank and Jacq acknowledge to one another with a glance that a kiss almost happened, and then back to Holly. "Okay, well we'll see you back at the seats then," Jacq says.

Frank and Jacq walk off into the nearest store, which is the bookstore they had already left. Holly watches them for a moment, and then continues on to the bathroom. She stops when a sudden jolt of pain strikes her stomach followed by a wave of pain down her legs. A couple passing by notices. "Are you okay?" the woman asks. Holly takes a few deep breaths and the pain fades away. She had almost gotten used to the stomach pain, which has come regularly since the first one on the plane, but the wave down the leg is new.

"I'm fine, thank you," Holly says. Not wanting to show her fear or cause a scene, she continues on toward the bathroom. The couple watches her with concern for a moment, but then walk away satisfied with her response.

With all the people scurrying around in the airport, the bathroom is oddly empty. Holly has used a stall and is now standing in front of the mirror touching up her makeup. She stops, looks down at her stomach, gently places her free hand to one side and says, "Now, I know you keep telling me you're ready to come out, but I'm asking you to wait a little longer, just one more day. Can you do that for me?" As if responding to the question, a sharp pain almost takes her to her knees. She pulls herself back up looking down at her stomach. "Okay, well then I'm telling you, as your mother, you are to stay put until we are in Arkansas."

In frustration, she shoves the makeup bag in the top of her suitcase and starts to march out. Before she breaches the doorway, water rushes from her crotch down the inside of both legs of her pants. She stops in shock and a bit of humiliation. "I didn't even feel like I had to go that time." With far less huff and a little extra fear, she turns back around and goes into a stall with her suitcase.

Outside the restroom, Frank and Jacq walk back out of the bookstore. They look around for Holly, but see that the coast is clear. They continue looking for more stores to go into, but quickly realize there aren't any more in this direction. Frank stops. "According to the signs, the only thing we'll find going this way is baggage claim or ground transportation," he says. They turn to walk back the other direction, but Jacq stops and turns back around.

"That's the answer," she says.

"What's the answer?" he asks.

"Ground transportation. It's exactly what we were just talking about, what Nellie was saying earlier. We should use

what's available to make this the best Christmas it can be.
All I've heard all day is that New York is the best place to be
at Christmas. If that's true, then what are we doing in New
Jersey? Let's go to New York!" she suggests excitedly.

Frank is taken aback. Go to New York? Now? He looks
at his watch. "It's 9:15 at night," he finally responds.

"Right," she says. "That should give us enough time to
get everyone together, out of here, and in the city well before
Christmas Eve becomes Christmas Day," she says.

"It sounds very exciting and spontaneous, which I love,
but I have a 7-year-old daughter who is already going to have
a hard time sleeping. Plus, I still have to find something to
replace the gifts she's not getting in the morning," he
explains.

"This IS the something that's going to replace those gifts.
Taking this trip into the city in the middle of the night is a
memory she'll compare every Christmas to after tonight,"
Jacq offers.

Frank admires the passion Jacq is emitting. "Look who's
found her Christmas spirit," he says with a laugh.

"Maybe. Either way, it sounds like a fun adventure
regardless what day of the year it is. I could use some more
fun in my life. But more than all that, it's the perfect gift for
Alonya," she suggests.

It's a great argument. He seems convinced, but then
shakes his head no. "I'd still need to buy something to cover
Santa's gift," he says.

"Not to spend all night quoting Nellie, but let Santa handle Santa's business," she suggests. Then she's struck by another idea. "Wait, this can be the Santa gift. We'll say he called you, that he arranged this trip into the city," she offers. "Give me your phone." He gives it to her. Jacq searches his call history to find her number from the call she made earlier. When she finds it, she saves her number, except she lists it as Santa. She then calls his cell from her cell so that it's the most recent call listed. "There. We're all set," she says while handing his phone back to him.

"Set to do what?" Frank asks.

"We'll go back and show Alonya that Santa called you. Then tell her that he's arranged for us all to go into New York City to celebrate Christmas," she explains.

Frank is reluctant. "I really appreciate you trying to help, but I'm not sure I'm comfortable lying to her," he explains.

"Who said anything about lying? Sure, we're regular human beings coming up with a plan, but where do you think that plan came from? The inspiration had to come from somewhere. I mean, here I am, a girl who didn't even want to discuss Christmas, now urging you to take a midnight Christmas tour. It's crazy. Or is it? Who's to say we're not just playing our part as Santa's helpers? The idea came through me, but I'm not all that certain it came from me. You were just looking for something to fill in for Santa's gift. This is the same thing," she closes her sales pitch showing her gleaming whites. He seems unconvinced, but then a look of happiness washes over his face.

"Let's do it!"

* * * * * *

119

Back at the gate, Alonya is seated next to Charley. They are playing with her stuffed animals, while Nellie enjoys a moment to shut her eyes. Charley is distracted from his play when he sees Holly walking back wearing a casual dress. "Why'd you change clothes?" he asks as she approaches.

"I don't know. Why do I do anything?" she retorts in attempts of avoiding a real answer. Before he has a chance to ask anything else, she diverts his attention by pointing to the stuffed dinosaur wearing a Santa hat that he's holding. "Who's your new friend?" she asks.

Charley turns to Alonya. "What did you say this little fella's name is again?"

"Her name is Dinah," Alonya says.

"Why did you name her that?" Holly asks, happy to be on a new topic.

Alonya shrugs her shoulders. "I don't know," she says. "That's just her name."

"Maybe because she's a dinosaur, and the first part of that is Dino, which is close to Dinah. Is that why?" Charley asks.

Alonya looks at him with a deadpan face, as if to say, *I have already answered that question.* She reaches over and takes Dinah back. Giving her a big hug she says, "I like her cause she's so soft."

"Hey everyone. We've got good news," Frank says as he and Jacq approach the group. "Santa has arranged a great trip for the lot of us as a special Christmas treat."

Everyone, including Alonya, looks at Frank as though he must have misspoke. "Is he going to fly us to Washington in his sleigh?" Alonya asks.

"No, we're definitely here for the night, but here doesn't have to mean here, if you know what I mean," he hints.

Holly frowns and furls her brow before saying, "I don't. What do you mean?"

"Well, Santa has organized for all six of us to go into New York for a late night Christmas tour of the city," he announces.

"Wow, that sounds neat," Charley says.

"We're going into New York City, tonight?" Alonya asks with great excitement.

Frank is thrilled with his daughter's response. It is just the kind of reaction he wanted her to experience when he set out to find a gift. "Yes, my sweet girl, we are. Get your animals packed up so we can go," he directs her.

Alonya quickly starts cramming her stuffed friends back into her suitcase. Charley looks around to see if she's missed any. Then he looks to Holly, who has become suspiciously quiet. "You okay?" he asks.

"Yeah. I'm great. Why?" she asks.

"You're just quiet is all. Do we need to pack anything up, or is everything ready?" he asks.

"Ready for what?" she asks before realizing what he's talking about. "Oh, do you want to go into New York?" she continues with the questions.

"Yeah. Don't you? You were all excited earlier when you found out we were so close. I figured you'd be chomping at the bit, especially if somebody else is paying," he says.

Holly searches for the right thing to say. "I was thinking it might be good for me to stay and rest," she finally says.

Frank overhears Holly. "You don't want to go? We'd really love to have you. I know Alonya has really connected with you guys. What can I do to convince you to come?" he asks.

"I'm just not sure I should do that much walking," she explains.

"We won't make you walk very much. We're going to take a bus into the city, and then we'll find a mini-van cab or something. Please come," Jacq urges.

"It does sound pretty cool, babe," Charley suggests.

Holly sees that she's outnumbered. She nods her head before saying, "Okay, let's go." Charley's smile broadens. He gets up and extends his hand to her. She gets up, and he helps her put her coat on. Frank helps Alonya with hers, too. With her standard independent spirit, Jacq slides into her new sleeping bag coat on her own. Everyone zips up and is ready to start walking when they simultaneously realize that Nellie hasn't moved from her seat.

"Aren't you coming, Nellie?" Frank asks.

"I think it'd be best if I stay here. My body has gotten used to Arizona winters, so there's no reason in shocking it with a Big Apple night scene," she explains.

"Like I told Holly, we'll keep the walking to a minimum," Jacq offers.

Nellie smiles but shakes her head no. "Thank you my darlings, but I think it's best that I stay right here," she answers.

Holly approaches with her hand on her belly and fear in her eyes. "Please come, Nellie. I'd feel so much better about going if you were there," she says. "With your former job and all," she adds.

"Yeah, all your years of singing in New York, I bet you have great stories you can tell us," Charley says.

Nellie realizes Holly is talking about her former years as a nurse. She takes a second look at Holly's hand on her belly, and then up to her eyes that are begging her to go. With an nod, Nellie stands up while saying, "Okay, let's go."

As the group of travelers arrives down on the ground transportation level, everyone turns toward the ticket counter for the NYC Shuttle. Jacq stops short when she notices someone outside the doors. "Hey guys, can you wait here for a minute?" she asks the group.

She walks outside and confirms that it is indeed who she thought it was. "Hey, aren't you the guy that was outside Port Authority this afternoon trying to get people to take a Christmas tour on your minibus?" she asks.

The guy looks at her for a moment before recognizing, "Oh yeah, Mrs. Scrooge. You didn't make it back here in time I'm guessing."

"Nope. I'm stuck for the night. What are you doing here? Tours wrap up for the day?" she asks.

"Yeah, turns out Christmas Eve isn't the best day to get people to take a tour. Everybody's either running around doing last minute shopping or trying to get to where they're going for the holiday," he answers. "I heard the airport shut down. Thought maybe some people would want to get out of here, but looks like I missed that rush too."

"So you're just standing out here waiting for someone who needs you to take them somewhere?" she asks almost not believing her luck.

"That pretty much sums it up," he responds.

"Santa or someone really must be in charge of this night," she says mostly to herself. "Okay, here's the deal. I have five adults and one child. We want you to take us into the city, give us the great Christmas tour you offered me earlier today, then have us back here before the airport opens in the morning. Deal?" she asks.

The guy can't believe his ears. "Um, yeah, but a deal normally concludes with an agreement on money," he responds.

"True," she acknowledges. "How much were you going to charge for the tour this afternoon?"

"Fifty bucks … but that was starting at Port Authority," he says.

"True, but that was also before your day was almost over and you were hoping to make up for a bad sales day," she says with a twinkle in her eye.

"Okay, fine. Six of you at fifty bucks a head, $300," he offers.

"One of those six is a child though," Jacq holds out.

"Come on, lady. I'm forgetting about the drive from here to the city, you can pay per head regardless of the age. Whatd'ya say?" he asks.

Satisfied with the negotiation, she says, "Deal. You get your minibus. I'll get my group."

Chapter 9

—————✳—————

The minibus is loaded up and driving Jacq and her fellow
travelers towards New York City. The interior seating is laid
out like a party bus so that all the passengers face each other.
There are three poles equal distanced from one another
running up the center. A small television is mounted in the
front left corner, behind the driver. And a much larger flat
screen television is mounted in the center of the back wall.
The seats and floor are black, while the poles and
embellishments are silver.

On this particular day, however, the minibus is decorated
with extra flair. The driver was after all planning to do
Christmas tours all day. Multi-colored rope lights hang
above the windows. They are also wrapped in a candy cane
effect on the three poles. Christmas music plays, a little too
loud, while the televisions rotate pictures of Christmas trees,
wreaths, and stockings.

The snowstorm that shut down the airport is still in full force. While residents of the northeast United States are used to going about their business in bad weather, this storm is exceptional. The roads are virtually empty, yet the minibus is moving about the speed one might on a busy weekday during rush hour.

Jacq is sitting closest to the driver on the passenger side so that it's easy for her to speak to him. Frank is next to her, and Alonya next to him. Across from them sits Holly, who is sitting between Charley and Nellie. Holly asks Jacq, "Do you think we can get him to turn the music down a little bit?"

Jacq in turn relays the messages to the driver, who didn't hear Holly, because the music was so loud. "Excuse me, can you turn the music down?" Jacq asks the driver.

"Sorry, I only have three options; on, off, or mute," he answers.

"Let's go for mute then," she chooses.

He nods, and hits the button that shuts the music off but keeps the pictures rotating on the television screens.

"Thank you," Nellie shouts out louder than needed for the now quiet bus.

"How did you score this again?" Franks asks Jacq.

"I met ... um," she stops with a realization. She looks to the driver and says, "I don't know your name."

"Antny," he says.

"Like an ant's knee?" Holly asks while pointing at her own knee.

"No," he responds. "It's Antny," he repeats as though it was clearer this time.

Holly looks at Charley to see if he heard a difference. He shakes his head. Looking in the rearview mirror, the driver sees that Holly is still confused. "Like Cleopatra's Antny," he explains.

"Like Cleopatra's what?" she asks.

"Oh," Charley interrupts. "It's AnTHony," he says.

"Yeah, exactly. Antny," Anthony confirms.

Jacq looks to see if everyone's clear before turning back to Frank. "So I met Anthony this afternoon. He was outside of Port Authority looking for tour patrons, and I was looking for the fastest way back to Newark," she explains.

"Then fate brought us back together outside said airport, and here we are driving into the city your lady there was so desperate to get out of," Anthony concludes. "Hey, is this who you were racing back to? This your husband and daughter ... um, I don't know your name either," he realizes.

"Jacq, but no this isn't my family. We're all new friends that met today on our flight from Phoenix," she answers quickly.

"Isn't it funny how that happens? Buddy of mine lives out in California. He'd lived in the same building for years, never knew his neighbors. That Northridge earthquake hit about four o'clock in the morning. By dinnertime, people who had never met one another were the best of friends. It works too. Some of those people have been close ever since. Hope the same happens for you guys," he adds.

Holly jolts to an upright position in her seat putting her hand on the top of her pregnant belly. She breathes hard for what seems like forever to her, but in reality is about forty-five seconds. By the time it's over, she looks up to see everyone's attention has turned to her. "Are you okay? Is the baby coming?" Charley asks.

"No, no," she responds. "It's just a little indigestion from all that airport food I've been eating today. I'm fine," she says.

"Didn't look like indigestion to me," Nellie says mostly to herself, but purposely loud enough for everyone to hear.

"Are you sure you're okay?" Jacq asks.

"I'm fine," Holly assures everyone. She looks around the bus at all the decorations. "Isn't there a large Jewish population in New York?"

"There is," Nellie answers. "My husband was Jewish. Why do you ask?"

"I was just wondering what they thought about Ant-knee's tour," she says. "I thought most people in big cities tried to stick closer to Happy Holidays so people didn't get offended if Christmas isn't the one they celebrate," she says to Anthony.

"True, but then there's been a big thing about people not wanting to feel oppressed about saying Merry Christmas or Happy Hanukkah," he answers.

"You've got the Merry Christmas crowd covered," Charley says.

"I've got the Hanukkah crowd covered too," Anthony says.

"Do you have another bus?" Alonya pipes in.

Anthony laughs. "Nope," he says. "I've got it all covered under this roof. Say a group wants to take a Hanukkah tour of the city. I hit this button here," he says as he flips a switch. The switch changes the red and green rope lights to blue and white. He flips another switch that changes the pictures on the televisions to rotating pictures of a menorah, a dreidel, and a Star of David. When he unmutes the sound, the system plays an instrumental Hanukkah song. "And I'd take you down to the lower east side by some historic synagogues, tenements, and then pop back up to 2nd Avenue Deli on 33rd for the perfect bowl of matzo ball soup."

"I've never had matzo ball soup, but it sounds good right about now," Holly says.

"We can do the Hanukkah tour instead if you want," Anthony offers.

"Let's stick with the Christmas tour," Jacq says. "But if you can fit some soup in, that would be great."

Anthony nods and switches the decorations back to Christmas. Jacq tugs on her ear, and Anthony mutes the music again. She looks over to Holly and asks, "Do you want soup now?"

"Oh I'm fine. I'm sure that'll change though. Never seem to know from one minute to the next what I'll want," Holly says.

"What's that?" Alonya asks her dad.

He looks ahead to where she is pointing and sees a long strand of tollbooths. To someone, like Alonya, who has never driven on toll roads, it looks strange to see the whole road blocked with this structure that cars are slowly driving through. "Those are the tollbooths," he replies.

The concept of a tollbooth, or a toll road for that matter, is fascinating to Alonya. "Do we have to pay to drive here because we don't live here?" she asks.

"No. Everyone that drives on this road pays," her father explains.

"Do they have to pay to drive on all the roads here?" she follows up her question.

"No. Just a couple I think," he answers.

"The turnpike and the parkway are the only two we deal with around here," Anthony adds.

"I'd drive on the roads that didn't charge if I lived here," Alonya concludes.

"Easier said than done," he answers. "You can do it, but it ain't easy."

Even with the conclusion that this is not a system that she'd partake in; she watches everything from her seat as cars slowly make it one by one through the booths. Because of the weather, there isn't much traffic. The minibus edges forward until it drives through the arched structure without stopping. "I thought you had to pay to go through there," Alonya says.

"I did," he replies. "It scanned my pass as I drove through."

This is even more fascinating to Alonya. The idea that money somehow magically changed hands without cash or even anyone speaking to each other is beyond her imagination. Yes, she's been with her dad at a gas pump, where neither cash nor talking to people are involved, but a card is swiped, and Frank does punch in numbers to approve the charge. Here, a car drives through. A laser scans something in the windshield, and payment is made. It's magic as far as Alonya is concerned.

"I wish I could do that at the grocery store," Holly says proving that it is equally fascinating to her. "That'd be great if you could just drive by and when you got home the groceries were sitting on the counter waiting to be put up."

"Why not just have them put up in the cabinets too?" Charley adds to the fantasy.

"Yeah, that'd be good too," Holly agrees.

"Look Dad!" Alonya screams out.

As the minibus makes its way to the Lincoln Tunnel, they can see the entire Westside of Manhattan. The night view of the lit up city is breathtaking. It's a sight that so many have seen in pictures, movies, and television; but to see it in person gives real life to those pictures. The top three tiers of the Empire State building are lit in red, white, and green.

The tiny lights that move along the boarder are cars driving on the Westside Highway, moving slower than normal, but still going.

"That's New York City!" Alonya announces.

Because everyone is mesmerized by the stunning view, only Nellie notices when Holly is struck by another contraction. Nellie checks the time on her watch. It's been ten minutes since the last one. She shakes her head in concern, but says nothing.

The minibus moves along through another set of tollbooths for the tunnel. Alonya is less enthused the second time around. She's still reeling from seeing the city. That excitement is then quickly replaced by entering the Lincoln Tunnel. The mile-and-a-half tunnel seems to go on forever, even though they are driving faster because they've momentarily left the weather restrictions behind. The lights change back and forth from bright white to more of a yellow shining against sections of the tiled walls.

It's nearing 10:30pm. Anthony drives quickly through the tunnel, but he slows down as they approach the tunnel's exit. There are signs of the snow again lying along the edges of the road. As they get closer to exiting, the snow grows inward on both sides toward the center until the whole road is white again. The air looks cold as the snow blows around under the blue white streetlights of 38th Street and 9th Avenue.

"Where's the Christmas stuff?" Alonya asks.

"Yeah, I thought everything would be red and green," Holly says.

"My dad said the first time he came here it was like driving into a sea of yellow from all the taxicabs. I don't see them either," Charley chimes in.

"Most of the cabbies are taking the night off, with it being the holiday and all. But you'll see some soon enough. There's not an hour in the day that New York City is without some cabs driving around. As for the red and green Christmas stuff, I promise ya it's coming," Anthony assures his passengers. "These are all apartments on this block. As soon as we get to the stores, you'll see tons of Christmas." He turns the minibus onto 8th Avenue, and drives up to 42nd Street next to Port Authority. He looks back at Jacq and says, "You were here just a few hours ago."

"Yes I was," she confirms. "What a difference those few hours have made," she says with a smile toward Frank. He reaches over and takes her hand. Alonya sees this. She doesn't say anything, but shows her approval by leaning in against her dad. He tucks her in under his other arm.

They drive east on 42nd Street. One block down from Port Authority, Anthony says, "Ladies and gentlemen, to your left is the world famous Times Square." They turn to see all the lit signs and billboards that advertise everything from delis, Broadway shows, and even underwear.

"Can we get out and see it?" Charley asks.

"We'll circle back around at the end of the tour. I'll get a good look at where the New Year's Eve ball will drop a week from now," Anthony says. "If you want, I can stop and let you get out then. It's going to be cold though."

He continues on 42nd Street across to 6th Avenue, where he makes a left to drive north. The signs of Christmas are more prevalent than when they first arrived into the city. Trees that line the avenue are draped with white lights from the ground to the tip of every branch. The detailed work for just one tree is impressive, but seeing the multitude of them coupled with the snow makes it feel like a true winter wonderland. As they continue up the avenue corporations have used the sides of their buildings to decorate. One has giant snowflakes flashing in multiple colors of white, blue, red, and green. Another has transformed a water fountain into a platform for a giant display of holiday lights that stand ten-feet tall. While on the next block, there is a life sized Santa with his gigantic sleigh and eight reindeer.

The minibus stops at a traffic light at the corner of 50th Street and 6th Avenue. Jacq vaguely remembers the intersection she walked across only a few hours ago. It all looks new to her. Granted, the night sky does highlight the festive bright colors better than before, but it's more than that. While she's seeing everything with the same eyes, it is with a new mindset. She's enjoying the moment she's in, versus trudging along desperately trying to get to somewhere else. What was a nuisance is now beautiful and awe-inspiring.

To their left is a display of red Christmas tree balls, but these aren't balls that could hang on any tree. Each ball is approximately seven-feet in circumference. There are ten balls stacked in a three-level pyramid, which stands somewhere around twenty-one-feet in the air. A few other balls are scattered around the main structure. All of this sits on top of a heated water fountain. With steam hovering above the water, coupled with lights reflecting mirrored images, and surrounded by the snow; the sight is nothing less than majestic.

Across the street, to the right of the minibus is the world famous Radio City Music Hall. Sitting above the venue's sign is a tree decorated only in lights standing somewhere between twenty and thirty-feet tall. An army of marching wooden soldiers surrounds the foot of the tree. "I have always wanted to go there," Holly exclaims with great excitement. "That used to be my dream. When I was in junior high school, I was going to grow up and become a Rockette. I can't believe I'm this close and still can't see them."

"Yeah, I'm pretty sure there aren't any more shows tonight," Jacq says. "They probably did their last show for the year earlier today."

"Nope," Anthony corrects Jacq. "They perform every day from early November until January 2. They'll even have shows tomorrow on Christmas Day, but you guys will be on planes heading out of here by then."

"Yes, we will," Nellie confirms.

Holly leans back in her seat. Nellie can see that she is fighting through another contraction, while everyone else's attention is on the views outside the bus. Nellie checks her watch, again. The contractions are maintaining ten minutes apart.

The traffic light turns green and the minibus continues up 6th Avenue. Jacq leans across Frank to Alonya to say, "The Radio City show has a live nativity scene. Do you know what that is?" Alonya shakes her head. Jacq explains, "Have you ever seen little figurines of Mary, Joseph, and baby Jesus? And, there are usually three wise men, and some animals; like camels, donkeys, and sheep. Have you seen that before?" Alonya nods yes. "That's a nativity scene.

Well, Radio City has real life animals in their show. How cool is that?"

"Is the real baby Jesus in the show too?" Alonya asks in all sincerity.

"No sweetie. They use actors for Mary, Joseph, and Jesus," Frank explains. "But it's pretty neat they have camels and donkeys here in the middle of such a big city."

"They live in the basement of the theatre for the run of the show. Early every morning, and then again late at night, the animals go for a walk on these very sidewalks. Wouldn't that be crazy to be walking down the street, and come across a camel?" Jacq says.

Alonya looks out the window. "I don't see any right now," she says.

"They're probably keeping warm tonight," Charley suggests.

Anthony drives his tour up to 59th Street, where he makes a right turn. Had he continued driving straight, he would've driven into Central Park. He explains to his passengers, "Normally, I'd take you through a bit of the park, but I'm not sure how clear the roads are in there tonight. Don't want to get you guys stuck. We're on 59th Street, which runs the whole way across Manhattan. This little piece of it though is also known as Central Park South. There are a lot of pricey homes to your right. Coming up we'll pass The Plaza Hotel, and then we'll make a right to head down 5th Avenue. Now, if you look to our left when we turn, you'll see FAO Schwarz, the toy store made famous by Tom Hanks in the movie "Big." Most people say Schwartz, but a real New Yorker knows the only T there is in the toys. And then, next door to FAO is the old home to the CBS Morning Show. Used to be full of people every morning, waiting for their chance to be on TV."

They arrive at 5th Avenue. Charley turns to see the famous toy store. Nellie whispers to Holly, "You need to tell him what's going on so we can get you to the hospital."

"I'm fine," Holly insists. "My mother was in labor with me for two days. She said the worst thing she did was rush to the hospital. They just wrote up a bill for seeing her, and then sent her back home."

"You are far from rushing to anywhere. And the safety of you and the baby is worth that bill," Nellie says.

Charley turns back around. "Honey, did you see the toy store?" he asks.

"Um, no. I was looking at the Plaza, where I want you to promise to take me one day," she replies.

As they drive down 5th Avenue, Jacq is mesmerized. "I can't believe I didn't see any of this earlier today. It's like I wasn't even here," she says.

"You were on this actual street?" Frank asks.

"Yeah, but I just wanted to get back to the airport. I was mad that my appointment had cancelled, that the car service couldn't come back early to pick me up, and that it was so cold. I was dressed in my cute little skirt and heels for the meeting, but never intended to be walking around outside. So, I was mad that I was even out there. All that madness prevented me from seeing all this great stuff," she says.

"They were though," Frank says.

"They were … here?" Jacq asks.

"Well, that too, but I was saying your little skirt and heels were cute. Got my attention," he says.

They stare into each other's eyes for a moment. It's brief, but it's a definite romantic connection. They're already holding hands, so they just grip a little tighter. Frank leans the opposite direction and kisses Alonya on the top of her head. He looks back out the window as the minibus continues down 5th Avenue. They pass stores like Bergdorf Goodman, Tiffany & Company, Elizabeth Arden, as well as famous buildings like Trump Tower. The lighting and displays are extravagant, but even more so, elegant. It's not just the sights are special. There's something in the air that is somehow tangible, even inside the minibus.

The minibus makes its way down 5th Avenue to 50th Street. Anthony pulls to the side of the avenue. "There's a lot of things here I don't want you to miss," he explains. "Obviously the easiest thing to see is the Rockefeller Christmas tree to our right." A long courtyard that dead-ends with the building now known to many as 30 Rock, frames the tree. It is easily 100-feet tall and lit with thousands upon thousands of lights.

"If you look a block behind us to your left, that's St. Patrick's Cathedral. And then directly across the street from us you'll see Saks Fifth Avenue," Anthony directs his tour. "I know they have stores all over the place now, but this is the one that actually sits on 5th Avenue. It's the real deal."

"That's where I bought my coat and boots earlier today," Jacq says.

"You shopped in there?" Alonya asks.

"I did," Jacq confirms.

"You're lucky," Alonya says mesmerized by the window displays.

Anthony starts driving again. At the end of the block, he makes a right on 49th Street. Driving just a short way down the street, he stops again. To their right is another angle of the Rockefeller tree. "So, if you look to your right, you get an even closer look at the tree, but if you look to your left you'll find a spot you may have seen on TV before. This is the home of NBC's Today show. Any given morning you can see Matt, Ann, Al, Natalie, and a host of celebrities," Anthony informs his tourists. "Across the street in the building behind the tree is where Saturday Night Live and Jimmy Fallon shoot their shows. It's also the former home to David Letterman, when he was on NBC, Conan O'Brien, when he was on NBC, the Rosie O'Donnell Show, and the original home of the Tonight Show starring Jack Parr, and then Johnny Carson before he moved it out to the west coast."

"To give you an idea of where we've been, we've circled back around to Radio City Music Hall. It's on the other side of Rockefeller Center," Jacq tells Alonya.

"It's another block up, but we're definitely close," Anthony says. "Next, I thought I'd drive us back over to the top end of Times Square. We should be able to find a deli or something open to get a nice hot bowl of soup. Then, I'll get you back out to the airport in plenty of time to get back through security and make it back to your gates so you can all spend part of your Christmas in your intended destinations."

"That sounds great," Frank says. "You want some soup?" he asks Alonya. She shakes her head no and nozzles up against her dad. "Someone's ready to sleep," he says. "I wouldn't mind some soup though."

"Sounds good to me," Charley agrees. He lays a hand on Holly's knee before asking, "You still in the mood for some?"

Somewhat noncommittal, she says, "Yeah, that would be nice."

Anthony drives them down 49th Street past 6th Avenue and over to 7th Avenue, where he makes a left turn. He drives two blocks down, and stops next to the TKTS booth, known to most as the half price booth for Broadway show tickets. "Just behind us at the top of the Olive Garden building is where the ball will drop almost exactly a week from right now," Anthony says.

"I want to get out," Charley says.

"Okay," Anthony replies. "Let me just officially park."

Mounds of snow pushed to the side of the road by plows ·block the only parking spaces on 7th Avenue. In his rearview mirror, Anthony can see a spot on 47th Street. On a normal day it would be impossible for him to get to it, but this is no normal day. He puts the minibus in reverse, and backs diagonally across the four lanes of 7th Avenue while turning onto 47th Street. As he edges the closer to the curb, the wheels slowly roll through the built up snow on the side of the road settling into a deep pile. They come to a stop with a slight drop and thud on the back passenger's side. It's not enough for a New York driver to be alarmed about, though. Anthony looks back to see his passengers are all looking toward him for an answer of what just happened. "It's nothing," he says. "Just a little pothole. If I were to get upset every time I found a pothole in this city, I'd never have time to be happy."

He opens the door. Jacq, Frank, Alonya, and Charley stand and start bundling up. Charley looks back to see that Holly and Nellie are still seated. "Aren't you two coming out?" he asks.

"I can see plenty right here in this warm bus," Nellie replies.

"What about you?" he asks Holly.

"It's so nice in here. I think I should stay with Nellie," she explains. "But you go on. Take some pictures with your phone."

He leans over to kiss his wife. "You sure you're okay?" he asks.

"I'm fine," she assures him.

Anthony leads the group off the minibus. Frank carries Alonya out. Though it's late, this seven-year-old has her eyes wide open so not to miss anything. They walk through the tire marks left from Anthony's parking job back across the avenue. Behind the ticket booth is a park of sorts with tables, chairs and benches for pedestrians. From this vantage point, they can see Times Square in every direction. Even with most of the businesses closed, this part of the city is lit up enough to simulate daytime. The white snow meeting the lights from all the signs makes the air look foggy. Alonya looks up and turns in every direction. "There's so much to see," she says.

"To finish up pointing out the morning shows, Good Morning America films a few blocks down on the left. You can see the ABC news feed down there," Anthony says.

Alonya opens her mouth to taste the snow. "Taste good?" Charley asks.

"It's cold," she says.

"I bet it is," he says before looking around at the mounds of snow. "Growing up in southern Arkansas, I never saw this much snow in my life." He gets a big smile on his face and then without warning, he takes off running. The group watch to see what he's up to. Charley spreads his arms open wide before leaping head first into a pile of snow. A puff of white hides him for a moment, but his heckle of laughter makes him hard to miss for long.

"I want to do that," Alonya says as Charley gets up.

"I'm not sure," Frank says. "These are the only clothes we have until we get to Washington."

Jacq laughs before she too takes off running without notice. Like Charley before her, she opens her arms wide and dives like the most elegant of birds taking flight. She lands softly in the cold powder. Her laugh echoes a sense of freedom she hasn't felt in a long time. "I would never do that," she screams out.

Alonya pats her dad on the shoulder insisting that he let her down to partake in the fun. He gives in saying, "One time."

Tucked back around the corner inside the minibus, Nellie and Holly sit quietly for a long while. A strain and pulling of the muscles rip across Holly's abdomen as another contraction strikes. She tries to hide it pretending to cough and hold her breath at the same time. Nellie looks at her watch. "Seven minutes," Nellie says.

"What?" Holly asks.

"Your contractions are down to seven minutes. It's not going to be long. You've given it a valiant try today, but this baby is not going to wait anymore than Jesus let Mary get back to Nazareth," Nellie says.

"I told you I'm fine," Holly says. "The baby's excited about Christmas like all of us, but he's going to be born at home."

"They say home is where your heart is. The shape of a big apple is similar to the shape of the human heart. The sooner you tell your husband what's going on, the sooner we can get you and the baby into the safest situation possible," Nellie says.

The door opens. Everyone except Anthony is covered in snow as they get back on the minibus. They are all laughing boisterously. "What did you do?" Holly asks, as light hearted as possible.

"You didn't see us? Honey, you missed it. We all dove face first into that snow over there. Well, everybody except Anthony," Charley says.

"It's hard enough for me to get out of a chair at my age. No reason to throw myself on the ground," Anthony explains. He reaches into a storage compartment above the passengers' seats and takes out a few hand towels. "It's no Ritz Carlton, but here's a little something to dry yourselves off with," he says has he hands the four snow covered passengers each a towel. "Now, I know I promised you guys soup from a deli, but it looks like we'll have to drive down a ways to find something open tonight."

Anthony sits down in the driver's seat. He left the minibus running to keep the heat on for Holly and Nellie. So, he puts it in drive, and ... nothing. The minibus won't move. He puts it in reverse, and likewise, there's a slight rocking, but no movement. He puts it back in park.

"Are we stuck?" Frank asks.

"It's nothing," Anthony says as he walks off the minibus. "Back in a minute."

Upon inspection, Anthony finds that the back passenger side is sitting a little lower than the rest of the vehicle. He tucks his gloves into his coat sleeves before digging snow away from the tire. The news is worse than he expected. The tire did go into a pothole like he suggested earlier. However unexpectedly, something popped the tire when that happened. It is now flat. Anthony shakes his head as he gets back on the minibus.

"Well folks, this is truly a special night for you. You are about to hear me say something that very few people get to hear," Anthony announces. He takes a moment before saying, "I was wrong. In this case, hitting the pothole was a big deal. We now have a flat tire."

"Oh no," Holly mutters.

"Not to worry my young mom to be. I'll have us out of here in no time. I just need to make a few calls to have someone come out to change the tire, but I promise to have you back at the airport in plenty of time," he says. "In the meantime, I should get you guys off the bus so fumes don't start to build up and such. I think the McDonald's around the corner on 7th is open 24/7. Why don't you all go have a cup of coffee on me?" he suggests.

Nellie turns around to look out the window. Across 47th Street, there is a blue metal door with one light bulb hanging above it. She stands and says, "I guess it's my turn."

"Your turn for what, Nellie?" Charley asks.

"Before Anthony showed up, I was supposed to be your tour guide. Well, come on," she says standing up. She looks at Anthony and asks, "You know the Blue Hideaway?"

"I've heard of it," he says.

"Do you know where it is?" she asks him.

"No," he replies.

"Then follow us before you start making your calls, so you'll know where to find us." She walks past everyone to the front of the minibus, and then off. "Come on. I can't be standing around in the cold," she calls out.

Everyone hurriedly bundles up and rushes out to follow her on their newest adventure of the night.

Chapter 10

Nellie leads her fellow travelers across the street from where the minibus is now out of commission. They pass the stage door to the Palace Theater, which has been home to Broadway shows like The Will Rogers Follies, Beauty and the Beast, and Aida to name a few. The next door down is a blue metal door with a light bulb hanging above it. There's nothing to stand out to the average pedestrian. There's no sign that directs any attention to it. Looking back to make sure the group has kept up, Nellie opens the door and ducks in out of the cold.

Inside, they enter a dark hallway lit with blue lights. Nellie pushes through a black curtain, and suddenly the group is standing in a grand room with oak panel walls and crystal chandeliers. Around the room are Vegas style booths with high backs covered in blue velvet that all face a stage. The stage sits dead center across from the entrance. Some of the greatest blues and jazz performers have entertained audiences for decades from that very spot. This night is no different. A trio of musicians is on stage playing "Merry Christmas Baby", setting the tone of the club.

The Blue Hideaway is a speakeasy, not just in name like many of the modern New York City clubs providing secret entrances to be hip. By the time prohibition went into effect in 1920, this club was in business hidden under the Palace Theatre, which was then home to the world's top vaudeville acts of the day. When prohibition ended in 1933, the club was such a trademark for amazing acts and good times that there was no reason to make it a storefront venue. So, the blue unmarked door remained the only hint of an entrance. If the light is on, that means the club is open.

This is the club where Nellie, as Stella Clark, gave most of her live performances. It is also the club where she and her husband gathered with all the blues and jazz musicians every Christmas Eve and gave the gift of music to one another well into Christmas morning. Tonight is Nellie's first time back since her move to Phoenix, but the sparse crowd is filled with many of the old regulars who have continued the tradition.

An old black man with a gray beard and mustache that matches the top of his head looks back and sees the group. He squints before his face shines with pure happiness and surprise. "Are my eyes lying to me, or did the great Stella Clark just grace our presence?" he calls out.

"Hello Clarence. It has been a long time, but you're looking good. Are you still running this place, or have you finally realized that it runs you?" she jabs fun at her old friend.

"Either way, we're still together in good times and bad, 'til death do us part," he replies before hugging her. "I didn't know you were in town. I would've sent a car to pick you up earlier before the storm got so bad."

"This is an unplanned stop. My friends and I got snowed into Newark during what was supposed to be a quick layover," she explains. "Our driver, Anthony, needs to get help with a tire. Do you mind if he uses your phone so not to spend any unnecessary time in that winter weather?" she asks.

"Of course," Clarence responds. "Come with me," he says to Anthony before turning back to Nellie. "Grab any open table."

"Oh, Clarence," she motions for him to come back over. When he does, she whispers in his ear, "I need you to pull some things together that I'm going to need shortly."

A waitress takes the rest of the group over to a booth. Nellie rejoins the group in time to slide in to the middle seat. The waitress says, "Hi Ms. Clark. It's so great to have you back home tonight."

"You don't look old enough to have been here when people knew who I was," Nellie says.

"You don't think I can work here and not know who Stella Clark is, do you? We're all excited to have a legend among us tonight," she says.

"That's very nice, but I tend to think one should be dead before referred to as a legend. If you need some formality, Mrs. Goldman will do, but you're welcome to call me Nellie," she suggests.

"Anything to make you comfortable Miss … Nellie. What can I get everyone?" she asks.

"We've been talking about soup for a while. Do you have any?" Holly blurts out.

"We actually have a special Christmas soup made with sausage and vegetables. Would you like that?" the waitress offers.

"I'll take the biggest bowl you offer it in," Holly says. There's agreement around that table that everyone will have the soup. The waitress leaves to fill the order.

"It must be hard to find musicians to take a job working so close to midnight on Christmas Eve," Charley says, referring to the trio who are just finishing their song.

"It's never hard to find a musician to take a job anywhere. Too many people want us to play for free. When a man calls with a check, a musician asks what time and where do you need me. But no one's getting paid here tonight. This is family night. It's where all the musicians and singers who didn't leave town for the holidays come to gather. If you even know the blues and you're without family in New York on Christmas, this is where you come," she says.

"Had you forgotten this was here?" Jacq asks Nellie.

"No," Nellie replies.

"If not for the flat tire, we were about to drive away," Jacq wonders.

"That's true," Frank adds. "Did you not want to come here?"

"It's not that at all. I've always loved coming here. That's just not the Christmas we were having. Bringing you here felt like taking you on a tour of my Christmases past. I was enjoying my Christmas present. But because of the tire, I get to have both," she explains.

"Ladies and gentlemen, can I have your attention," Clarence says from the stage. "Now, I know she wants to sit over there and pretend she's a regular person named Nellie, but Stella Clark will always be one of the greatest stars that has ever shined in this club. She and her husband, Mr. Albert Goldman, were mainstays here for many, many years. I know some of you benefited from the masterful music management of good ole Albie Goldman. He's gone on to be with the angels now, but tonight those angels have blessed us with a real Christmas treat. Our star is home. Everybody put your hands together and help me encourage the great Stella Clark to come up here and share a song with us."

Nellie smiles knowing she wouldn't get through the night without singing a song in here. Frank, Jacq, and Alonya stand to let her to get out of the booth. She makes her way to the stage, and confers with the pianist before taking the microphone. "Merry Christmas everyone. I woke up in Phoenix, Arizona this morning with no idea that I was going to be in New York City by the end of the day, but here I am. And, here it goes." She motions with a swing of her hand for the pianist to start. He strikes a blues chord, and she begins singing "Silent Night" a cappella. Her voice echoes through the room with a smooth comfort. Other than her voice the room is completely silent. The wait staff has stopped working. The kitchen staff has left their posts, and come into the main room. People are holding their breath to retain the moment. She reaches the end of the first verse with "sleep in heavenly peace." Silence fills the room. Everyone sits still enjoying the lingering tones that still waft through their heads. If she were to walk off the stage right now having sung only that, people would talk for years about it being one of the best things they ever experienced, but of course there's more.

The pianist kicks back in with a stunningly beautiful and uplifting blues version of the song that brings new life into the room. Nellie matches the spirit and sings of silence with a celebratory tone that gives great peace.

"Oh my gosh, that sounds even better than your record," Holly says to Charley. "Record it with your phone."

Charley takes his cell phone out of his pocket. He pulls up the camcorder app, and starts recording. Holly decides she has a better angle from where she is sitting, so she takes the phone from her husband. Another contraction hits, but Holly holds strong. The only real indication of it is a jolt in the video footage when her hand shakes while holding the phone.

Next to them, Alonya is so excited to see and hear Nellie on stage. If her smile were any bigger, her lips would be touching her ears. Her eyes are wide open as though she's just learned of the greatest surprise. She doesn't want to miss any part of this magic moment. "You like hearing Nellie sing?" Frank asks his daughter.

"It's the most beautiful thing I've ever heard," she replies without taking her eyes off the stage.

Frank leans the other direction toward Jacq and asks, "How do you feel about Christmas now?"

With a look of tenderness, she looks in his eyes not wanting to miss a moment either. Her smile grows a little bigger, and then without a word she leans in and kisses him. It is a soft lip to lip kiss that lingers for a few extra seconds. They break apart. "Wow," is all he can say.

"Wow is exactly what I was thinking," she replies.

He turns to see how Alonya is reacting to seeing her dad kiss another woman. She is still locked on Nellie, and missed it completely. They turn back to the stage, where Nellie has full control of the room. When the song comes to an end, the audience leaps to their feet with applause.

Clarence comes back on the stage. He takes the microphone and says, "It's so good to have you home. Miss Stella Clark, everyone!" The continued applause grows louder. As the audience slowly takes their seats, Nellie walks off the stage. "Will you sing another?" Clarence asks.

"A little later," she confirms before excusing herself to the ladies room.

Back at the table, Holly is excited to see what she captured on the phone. "I hope the picture is good," she says. "We should post it on YouTube." She pushes a button to pull up the video, but instead opens Charley's text messages. The last text he received from his friend from work pops up. "Why do you need to be dead or really sick?" she asks.

Charley, who was looking around the room, jerks around. "What? What are you doing?" he asks reaching to take the phone from her, but it's too late.

She's already pulled up the text from his boss. "You're fired?" she announces in full shock. "How could you not tell me that you got fired? What did you do?"

"We're going to give you guys a few minutes," Frank says as he motions for Jacq to get up.

"No Frank. Ya'll stay here. I've got to get up," Holly says. Charley stares at her shell-shocked. "Get up," she orders him.

Charley scoots out of the booth. He turns to help her up, but Holly refuses his assistance. She gets up on her own and heads over to the bar. Charley dutifully follows. "Sweetie, I'm sorry I didn't tell you. I was going to wait 'til after Christmas," he says.

"How could they fire you? I thought you were doing good," she says.

"I was."

She stares at him waiting for more of an answer. "You were until what, when?" she asks. He struggles to gather the right words. "Just say it. What happened?" she asks again.

"I didn't have permission to take today off," he blurts out. "But you were so unhappy … I just couldn't let you be that miserable on your favorite holiday. So, I booked our tickets and left town."

"And they fired you? Because of me?" she asks as she begins to cry.

"It wasn't because of you," he says while caressing her head. "I had a choice to make, and I made one. That choice got me fired."

"That choice was because of me. It's my fault. I got you fired. How are we going to pay for the baby, or us, without your job?" she wonders out loud.

Anthony walks by them. "Hey, don't cry. I'm going to get the tire changed out, and the bus will be back on the road in no time. You'll see," he offers. "I'm on my way out there now to meet the guys."

"Can I come?" Holly asks.

"Um, you can, but wouldn't you rather stay warm in here? Maybe that Stella Clark will sing another song. Who knew I had Stella Clark on my bus?" Anthony says.

"I need to get some air. Do you mind if I walk with you to the bus?" she asks again.

"Sure, you guys can come if you want," he answers.

Holly looks at Charley. "I just need a few minutes to clear my head, figure out what to do," she says.

"We'll figure it out together. We need to figure it out together. It's our life, our family," he says.

"I know. You are a great husband, probably better than I deserve. You're going to be a great father too. I'll sit down with you and figure it all out in a bit, but first I need a few minutes to pull myself together," she says.

"Honey, it's cold outside. I don't think it's good for you or the baby," he says.

Holly holds up a finger to Anthony asking him to wait a minute for her. She walks back over to the table. "Jacq, would you lend me your coat? I'd like to go out to the bus with Anthony, but Charley is worried it's too cold outside for me and the baby," she asks.

Without question, Jacq takes it out from under her and gives it to Holly. Holly nods towards Charley as she puts the coat on. "I'll be nice and warm now. Ten minutes?" she asks.

He gives up. "Yeah, do what you need to do."

Outside, Holly and Anthony walk back out onto 47th Street. The wind has picked up carrying the snow from the ground into swirls in the air. For Holly, it feels like she's put on an oxygen mask. Thoughts rush through her mind. She should've told Charley that she's in labor. Why is she hiding it from him? She cost him his job? Where will they live? Should they move back to Arkansas? What would they do there? The whole reason for moving to Phoenix was because it was a far better job than Charley could get if they stayed home. What was she going to do? No, Charley was right. It was a "they" problem. What were they going to do? Why did Charley pacify her with this trip if it was going to jeopardize their family's future? What was he thinking?

She looks up and down the street. The only real movement is the traffic lights getting pushed around a bit from the wind. "Is it okay if I sit on the bus 'til the guys come to change the tire?" Holly asks Anthony.

"Yeah, sure. We may need to have you get back off when they jack up the bus, but it's fine 'til then," he says. He takes his key out, and opens the door for her.

Holly enters the minibus. She leans her head against the first pole she comes to. Tears roll down her cheeks. She uses her hand to wipe her face dry. Another pain strikes her stomach. Her knees weaken. This contraction is different. A second stronger contraction starts almost before the first one finishes. Holly moves to sit, but finds it hard to move her feet because a pain shoots from the middle of her back down her legs to the bottoms of her feet. She stumbles, but catches the second pole to prevent the fall. She looks out the window, but Anthony is looking the other direction and can't see her.

Back inside the Hideaway, Nellie comes back to the table. Charley is sitting on the edge of the booth looking away. Frank and Jacq are holding hands enjoying the music, while Alonya sleeps against her father's side. Nellie sits on the other side of the booth without saying anything. She just looks toward the stage to enjoy the music herself. Alonya stirs awake. She looks around the booth twice. She takes her dad's arm to look at his watch. It's a few minutes until midnight. She looks around the booth and then the room again. "Where's Holly? It's almost Christmas Day. We should all be together," she says.

Frank enjoys the sweetness of his daughter. "She's okay. She wanted to walk out to the bus with Anthony," he says.

"How long have they been gone?" Nellie asks.

"Maybe ten minutes," Charley answers.

"I think we should go out there. They shouldn't be alone when Christmas starts," Alonya says.

"They're fine," Frank assures her. "It's not like New Year's Eve when we celebrate the clock striking midnight."

"I think your baby girl is right," Nellie says. "We need to get back to the bus. Charley and I will take off. Frank, will you ask Clarence to give you the stuff I asked him to prepare?"

"Sure, is everything okay?" Frank asks.

"Of course it is," she answers unconvincingly.

Back at the minibus, Holly is having a hard time holding it together. She can't pull off the façade any longer. Everything in her being is letting her know that the baby is on the way out. Another contraction strikes. Holly bangs her palm against the window before sliding off the bench onto the floor. Anthony runs onto the minibus.

"Are you okay?" he asks.

"Baby. The baby's coming," she says. "Can you go get my husband?"

Right on cue, Charley and Nellie come onto the bus. "I had a feeling we'd find you like this," Nellie says.

Charley dives down on his knees. He brushes Holly's hair out of her face with his hands. "Are you okay? How long has this been going on?" he asks.

"All day," she replies.

"You've been in labor all day? Why didn't you tell me? I would've taken you to the hospital instead of the airport," he replies.

"No, I got the first pain on the flight here. I was trying to hold out until we got home, but it doesn't look like our little one wants to do it that way," she says.

Alonya runs on to the bus. "Are you having your baby?" she asks excitedly.

Frank and Jacq come on behind her carrying a cardboard box filled with a stack of clean towels, a box of plastic kitchen gloves, a pair of scissors, and a bottle of rubbing alcohol. "Is this happening now? Are we doing this here? Should I call 911?" Frank asks concurrently.

"Yes, that's a good idea, the last one about calling 911," Nellie clarifies. "But I suspect we may have a baby here before they arrive." She looks at Charley. "It's okay though. We're going to do this together. Sit next to Holly. Your job is to help her breath and keep her calm." She looks back at Frank and Jacq. "I'm going to need your help. You can ask Clarence to watch Alonya in the club. She'll be safe in there," Nellie suggests.

"No, I want to stay," Alonya asks.

"The adults need to do something really important right now," Frank tells her.

"Please don't make me go," Alonya pleads. "We should all be together with the baby when it turns to Christmas."

Frank is at a loss. He sees that Holly needs everyone's help, but he doesn't want to abandon his daughter either.

"Can we have Alonya sit on the other side of Holly? I think she'll do a fine job of keeping the mother calm," Nellie suggests. Under her breath she adds, "And it will keep her from seeing everything."

Frank agrees. Alonya hops over and sits on the floor next to Holly. She pats Holly's shoulder. Nellie takes the scissors and cuts Holly's dress up to the waist. "Lift your legs up for a minute, baby," she asks Holly. Holly does as requested. Following Nellie's lead, Jacq helps spread the clean towels under Holly from her waist down. There are now three layers between the floor and where the baby will arrive – the towels, the cut dress, and Jacq's new, white sleeping bag coat. She and Holly come to the realization about the coat at the same time.

"I'm sorry. Do you want me to take it off?" Holly asks Jacq.

"No, not at all. Consider it your first baby gift," she replies.

"Go ask Anthony to get the engine running so we can have some heat in here," Nellie instructs Frank. He hops off the minibus. Nellie stands up, and takes her coat off. "I'll give you a lot of things, but this coat is not one of them," she tells Holly with a glimmer in her smile. Nellie proceeds to take off all her jewelry, and rolls up her sleeves to her elbow. She opens the bottle of rubbing alcohol and pours it in her hands. She then rubs it up both arms. Without a word, she hands it to Jacq. "Do what I just did," Nellie instructs her as she puts on a pair of the plastic gloves.

The guys come back on the minibus. Frank told Anthony what's going on, but seeing it in person is still shocking.

"She's going to give birth right here on my bus?" he asks. "Wouldn't it be better inside the club?"

"It would be better inside a hospital, but right here is where it's going to happen," Nellie says. "Can we get some heat going?" Anthony does as requested.

Jacq has followed Nellie's lead and is alcohol clean to the elbows with her plastic gloves on. "I'm ready to assist you," she tells Nellie.

"Get ready to assist Holly," Nellie says. "These knees are almost 80-years-old. I'm lucky to have done what I already have."

Jacq thought she was shocked before, but she just found a new depth of surprise in her. "I don't know how to deliver a baby," she proclaims.

"I do, and I'll be sitting right here telling you what to do," Nellie explains.

Before Jacq can protest any further, Holly screams out in pain. She grips Charley's hand so tight that he grimaces. Alonya strokes Holly's other arm. "You're going to be okay," she says.

"The baby will be here any time," Nellie says.

"Doesn't her water have to break first?" Charley asks.

"It broke a few hours ago," Holly finally admits.

He's upset to learn that she kept this from him, but is overjoyed by what it means. "We're about to become parents," he says.

161

Holly's smile is quickly lost when another pain rolls in. The contractions are coming faster and lasting longer. She screams out again. "I'm sorry," she then says to Alonya. "I don't want to scare you."

"It's okay. You're just calling out so the baby knows which way to come," Alonya suggests.

"I never thought of that, but I bet it does help," Holly responds. She looks the other direction at Charley. "I'm sorry I've been such a pain about Phoenix. Of course it was the right move for us. It'll give our baby the best possible future. Can you get your job back?"

"Since you're having the baby, I can probably claim a medical emergency … the New York part's going to be hard to explain though," he teases her. "Seriously though, stay focused on our baby right now. The rest will work itself out."

"I have a support system there now," she says indicating the group surrounding them.

Another contraction comes. Holly jolts upright. Nellie slides across the bench seat to help settle Holly back. Holly looks up at her. "Your singing was so beautiful tonight. I've heard good singers before, but I've never had anything touch me like that," she declares.

Nellie begins humming "Silent Night" to calm Holly. The hum is guttural and soothing. It's the kind of healing sound that comes straight from the soul. Holly breathes easy for a moment.

Jacq's jaw drops when she glances toward the window. "What is that?" Everyone turns to see a camel looking inside the minibus.

Frank and Anthony go outside. The camel is standing next to the minibus with a leash hanging free. It looks at Frank, but then turns back to look inside the window. From the other direction, a man runs up. "I'm really sorry," the man calls out. "He got away from me. It's never happened before." Behind him, is another man running with two donkeys on leashes.

"Really?" Frank exclaims.

"We're animal wranglers for Radio City," the man explains. "The snow eased up, so we were taking a few of the animals out for their nightly walk. He got away from me. It's never happened before," the first wrangler says again.

About this time, the tow truck pulls up with a yellow light flashing. Anthony goes over to talk to the driver. It's going to be a little while before they can change the tire. The wrangler notices that the truck hasn't spooked the camel, nor has he tried to run away anymore. "What's going on here? Do you need any help?" The second wrangler, with the two donkeys makes it to the minibus. Behind him, is a third wrangler dragging a couple of sheep along as he runs to catch up.

Frank shakes his head in disbelief. "Um, there's a lady having a baby inside. I'm not sure whether your camel is distracting her in a good or bad way, but I'm sure he's taking her attention off the contractions, at least a little," he says.

"That is crazy. Like I said, Ted has never gotten away from me before. But it was like he knew where he was

going. We walked across 6th Avenue, and then he just broke
free. These guys," indicating his fellow wranglers, "were
trying to help me, but could only run so fast with their
animals in tow. I didn't know what I was going to do. I
couldn't catch up to Ted and none of the signals we use were
working either. He was ignoring everything I did. Then, he
just stopped here at this bus," the wrangler says.

"Crazy is definitely a good description," Frank agrees.

Alonya pops her head out of the doors. "Daddy, Daddy,
come meet the baby." Frank goes back inside. The
wranglers don't rush away. Curiosity has them hooked.
Inside, Frank walks in to see Charley nuzzled up to Holly
with his arm around her. She is holding their new son, who
is swaddled in some of the clean towels. "His name is Nick,"
Alonya announces.

"After St. Nicholas?" Frank asks.

"Oh yeah, it works for that too," Holly says. "But no, he's
named after Phoenix, this little man's hometown. And his
middle name is York, because this is where everything
changed for us. Nicholas York Carpenter," she announces.

"That sounds like a fine name for a boy who will grow to
be a distinguished man," Nellie responds.

Their voices are drowned out for a moment when the
ambulance arrives with the siren blaring and the red lights
flashing. Through the window they can see Anthony
greeting the paramedics. The ambulance has gotten the
attention of the Blue Hideaway patrons and drawn them out
on the street. It's starting to look like quite the scene with
red and yellow lights flashing from the trucks, Radio City
nativity animals wandering about, and blues musicians who

begin to celebrate when they hear the news by playing "Go Tell it on the Mountain."

Alonya grabs her dad's wrist to read his watch. "It's after midnight. Merry Christmas everyone!" She hugs up against her dad's side. He puts his arm around her, while reaching over to pull Jacq next to him under his other arm. Nellie pulls her coat back over her shoulders and settles onto a seat to relax. Charley embraces Holly, while their new baby boy nuzzles against her chest. This is a night of new beginnings, of budding friendships, relationships, and family. The gifts have been far too great for wrapping paper and bows. While the clock will continue to move forward, and the travels will start anew, this moment will linger for years to come. It is the merriest of moments. It is a very Merry Christmas.